Bee Keeping for Cats

Peter Tye

In memory of Larry, a devious, vicious cat who punched well above his weight and provided the template for Lettuce, the blood thirsty tabby.

With thanks to Marc Heraud who gave me the title and a blank manuscript!

PRIVATE
&
CONFIDENTIAL

BUZZ OFF!

This file is on the family computer, guarded by a fiendishly clever encoded password. If you are reading this confession, it can only be because:-

- I have succumbed to a long period of relentless torture.
- I have suffered a fit of remorse and decided to reveal my guilty secrets to the world.
- I have come to an untimely end and a feline friend has released this file in search of justice. Whatever the reason, this confession has found its way into the public domain and the information contained herein will solve a catalog of diabolical crimes. For I am - or was - a cold calculating killer!

Sorry tabby fans, but it's true.

CHAPTER ONE: SEEDS OF EVIL

I'm not sure where it all started. Perhaps it was when they named me 'Lettuce'! I ask you, what sort of a name is that for a kitten descended from a long line of carnivores? It was plain for all to see that I had all the characteristics of my 'Big Cat' cousins, but not to Toby and Jessica. Toby, bought me as a birthday present for Jessica, shortly after their marriage. She was in the kitchen, preparing a salad, when Toby presented her with a gift wrapped cage, tied with a pink ribbon. I was inside, sitting in the dark, wondering what was going on.

Then the wrapping came off and I saw Jessica smiling at me. I was confused, especially when she called me 'Lettuce'. Later she claimed it was the salad which made her think of Lettuce. Perhaps I should be grateful; I could have been, Cucumber, Tomato, Beetroot, Onion, Radish, or even - Hard Boiled Egg!

I missed the playful rough and tumble of the kittens in the pet shop and to compensate, Toby bought a collection of playthings for me. Balls, furry toys, dangling toys, wind-up toys, feathery toys on springs, a play tunnel - and that was just for starters! Both he and Jessica spent many hours encouraging me to pounce and catch. but inevitably, there were long periods when I was alone. Sometimes I would play with the toys, but it wasn't the same as wrestling with a live kitten.

Then, one day, as I was grumpily looking at all my toys, hoping one would spring into life, something moved!

Up near the ceiling a small black object was moving quickly along the top of the curtain rail. I jumped onto an armchair to get a closer look. It stopped to look down at me, then ran back the way it came. It wanted to play! Aiming for the rail I took a flying leap from the back of the armchair, but fell woefully short of my target.

As I hit the curtain, my claws automatically flicked out and I clung on. Then, paw over paw, I climbed up towards the curtain rail and my new found play mate. Well, that's what I intended, but my claws cut through the curtains and I slowly sliced my way down to the floor. Jumping onto the armchair, I launched myself at the curtains again - again - and again.

Eventually there were no curtains left to cling to, and my playmate had disappeared. It was time for a snooze.

When Jessica returned home, the first thing she usually did was make a fuss of me - but not on that day. She took one look at the curtains and shrieked, "Lettuce!" She picked me up roughly. "Bad Lettuce! Bad Lettuce!" She pushed my face into the shredded curtains and screamed. "No! No! No!"

How was I supposed to answer. I looked at her wide eyed and gave a pathetic little mew. It seemed to work, for she gave me a kiss, apologized for shouting at me, but said I had been very naughty and Toby would be very cross. Then she began to shout for him.

"Toby! Toby! Toby!"

Toby rushed into the room. "What's wrong? What . . ." He broke off, staring at the shredded curtains. "Oh my God!"

"No, not the curtains - there!" Jessica pointed towards my play tunnel. "In there! It ran in there! An enormous spider!"

My playmate ran out from the other end of the tunnel, made a fast right turn and scuttled towards the television.

So that's what it was; a spider, but hardly enormous, nowhere near as big as a kitten. Jessica hugged me protectively to her bosom as the spider disappeared from view.

"Do something about it, Toby!" There was genuine panic in her voice.

"What, the spider or the curtains?" Toby grinned at me. "You're a naughty little kitten." He wasn't cross at all. He gave Jessica a sympathetic smile and put his arm around her shoulder. "Come on, let's go into the kitchen. I'll catch the spider later."

I sat on Jessica's lap while they had tea. They were laughing about the curtains by that time.

The following day, I was alone in the living room again. The curtains still hung in tatters, but there had been talk of replacing them and whether or not they could be made 'kitten proof'. Toby had not found the spider, so I was hoping it would come out to play. I kept half an eye on the curtain rail as I whacked my bright red bird toy around the room.

I called the bird Dipper and if the spider ever returned it would be Scuttler. Dipper had been whacked to all corners of the room before Scuttler made an unusual entrance, swinging down from the curtain rail on a single thread.

I kept my excitement in check as the spider dropped closer. Then judging the time right, I jumped onto the back of the armchair and performed, what I would later call, my aerial pounce! Scuttler never stood a chance, but, when I opened my paws on landing, there was no spider! I looked around the floor. It was nowhere to be seen, then, out of the corner of my eye I saw something moving. Scuttler was climbing swiftly back up the thread. He was going to be a great playmate and catching him would be a real test. Climbing the curtains was obviously out of the question, I had to think of something else. Time for another snooze.

The cheek of it! Scuttler ran past my nose and into the play tunnel. Instantly awake, I scampered over to the tunnel and poked my head in.

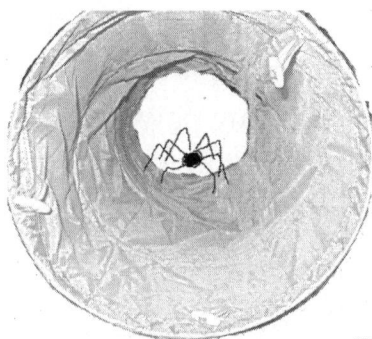

There it was, scuttling along the bottom of the tunnel. I moved stealthily to the other end and paw raised waited for it to reappear. But it fooled me by climbing out through a play hole and scuttling back along the roof of the tunnel. I pounced! The tunnel collapsed! Scuttler was thrown off, but landing on all legs headed at great speed for the kitchen door. I scrambled over the play tunnel, lunged forward and managed to place a blocking paw. Scuttler executed a ninety degree turn. I blocked with my other paw. Scuttler turned to face me, then rather cheekily, made another turn and ran up and over my paw. I let the spider think it was getting away, then, on a count of three, I pounced! I could feel the legs scrabbling under my paw - then nothing. Cautiously I lifted my paw to check. The spider was there, but to my dismay the legs had disappeared. Scuttler had turned into a black ball.

I gave it a push and it rolled away. I pushed in the opposite direction and it rolled back. I quickly came to the conclusion that without legs to scuttle around with, a spider is not much fun.

I wedged the black ball between two claws and threw it high into the air. It bounced silently on the floor. I threw it higher and caught it in my mouth. Something went pop, it tasted bitter. I spat it out! The legs slowly reappeared and I urged Scuttler to get up and run - to continue our game, but, nothing happened. I pushed Scuttler around for a short while, then returned to Dipper. Dipper's spring worked perfectly, time after time.

I was dozing when Jessica and Toby arrived home. Panic! I had forgotten to hide the evidence!

Scuttler's body was in full view as Jessica came into the room. I braced myself for more hysterical screams, but none came. Instead, she picked me up, gave me a kiss and told me how clever I was.

Toby was called to dispose of Scuttler, and I was taken into the kitchen to receive some of the best treats known to cat-kind.

As I crunched through them I wondered if I should feel a pang of guilt, but I felt nothing. I had become . . . a paid assassin!

CHAPTER TWO : MEETING THE PRINCE OF DARKNESS.

Jessica and Toby's house was in what they called suburbia. It was a semi-detached property in a street which seemed to go on forever.

A week after the Scuttler affair I was given access to the whole of the house. Toby told me it was because I was house trained, but I believe it had a lot to do with the fulfillment of the Scuttler Contract. Upstairs, two things immediately appealed. The large comfy bed, and the view from their bedroom window. All the houses had long rear gardens, which backed onto those of the houses in the next street. When darkness fell this enormous space became a battleground for creatures of the night - especially cats

As I looked out over the sunlit gardens that first time, everything looked peaceful, if not particularly well ordered. Strips of lawn were interspersed with jungles of vegetation and sheds of all shapes, sizes and degrees of dilapidation. The gardens were divided by a dislocation of wood panel fences, brick walls, concrete blocks, trimmed hedges, overgrown hedges and horizontal sheets of rusting corrugated iron. In that higgledy piggledy melange, something moved! A black shape leaping confidently over fences and walls and squirming through hedges, until it emerged on top of the wall which divided our garden from that of our immediate neighbor.

It was a large black cat, ugly as sin; bloated cheeks, ears with chunks missing, a scraggy bent tail, and enormous front paws This pugilistic creature confidently rolled over onto its back to enjoy the sunshine. Then, it saw me! In an instant it was on its feet, stalking menacingly along the wall. I backed away from the window and fortunately, fell into Jessica's waiting arms.

"What have you seen out there darling?" She had taken to calling me, Lettuce darling, darling Lettuce, and sometimes, just darling. She kissed the back of my head and followed my gaze down to the wall, where the black cat was baring its teeth at me.

"Nothing to worry about, Lettuce darling, It's Vince from next door, a bit of a rough diamond, but his heart's in the right place. Look, he's smiling; he wants to be your friend."

I didn't think so. Vince may have been showing lots of teeth but his ghastly yellow eyes were sending out a different message. A message of hate, evil, and intent to maim. I was rather pleased when Jessica moved away from the window and sat down on the big squidgy bed. She told me it would be sometime before I could be allowed out in the garden, but that did not bother me. I was happy with the new freedom I had indoors, and content to look out from the bedroom window, watching the comings and goings of Vince and eventually, steeling myself to stare back into those dreadful yellow eyes.

Vince began to leave dead birds, mice, moles and rats on the garden wall, just beneath the bedroom window. Jessica saw it as friendly act. I saw it as a warning sign. Vince wanted me to be in no doubt that he was a deadly killer.

*****

The sudden noise almost made me jump out of the litter tray - which could have been very nasty! I hastily finished what I was doing and went from the utility room into the kitchen to investigate.

Toby was drilling a hole in the back door. I kept a safe distance and watched as he drilled hole after hole. He turned and grinned at me. "This is for you Lettuce." He gave the door a hefty kick and a chunk of it fell out onto the patio leaving a big square hole. Wow! What had he done? I wouldn't want to be in his shoes when Jessica came home! But Toby seemed quite unconcerned as he used a saw to tidy the edges - then he said it again!

"This is for you Lettuce."

So that was his little game. He had made the hole in the door to get me into trouble! Time to make myself scarce.

I was at the top of the stairs when Jessica came in through the front door. I watched her walk through to the kitchen, and waited for the explosion – but none came. Instead, she called sweetly up the stairs for me. "Lettuce! Lettuce! Kitty - Kitty - Kitty. Come on Lettuce darling, we've got something to show you." She didn't seem angry, so I took a chance and went down the stairs to meet her. She picked me up and carried me into the kitchen. The hole in the door had been covered by a sheet of plastic. Toby was nowhere to be seen, which did not surprise me.

Then, Jessica crouched down and pushed my nose against the plastic. I remembered how she had pushed my face into the shredded curtains. She was cross after all! She pushed harder. Hey! This was going to hurt!

"You've got your own little door now, Lettuce," she said. Then the plastic gave way and I found myself out on the patio, where Toby pushed me back through again. Then Jessica pushed me out. Then Toby pushed me back. Then Jessica pushed me out. Then Toby.... "Hey, that's enough! I've got the message." I wriggled, turned, gave Toby a severe nip on the thumb, and when he dropped me, ran off down the garden. Panic ensued! Jessica ran after me. I dodged into the flower border. She followed. I wriggled through a dense jungle of long stemmed plants. She called for Toby, who was sucking blood from his thumb. I ran out between her legs, across the lawn, into a rose bed. Toby made a lunge for me, pushing his wound free hand through a rose bush. He called me a name, which I could not possibly repeat and raised a clenched fist, dripping with blood, threatening all sorts of dreadful retribution.

I broke cover, sprinted back across the lawn and climbed an apple tree, which, I have to say, was much easier, and rewarding than climbing curtains.

There was a brief moment of panic when it looked as if Toby would catch me, but a frantic scramble took me up into a fork in the tree and out of reach. From there it was easy to walk along a branch, which stretched out over the neighboring garden. Jessica called for me to come down, but I nestled into a comfortable spread of leafy twigs and refused to budge. Eventually I heard Toby say he had to attend to the wounds on his hands and they both left.

"Nice one, dude."

I peered down through the leaves, and froze. Vince was on the garden wall only a couple of feet below, those dreadful yellow eyes looking up at me. He spoke in what I would later recognize as an American accent.

"Heh! Heh! Yup, that was a nice one, Little Buddy. Now, while you're over there - over ma territory, and I'm here, on what should be no cat's land, except I've claimed it as ma own, I'm gonna tell ya how the land lies."

An enormous black paw appeared through the leaves, inches from my face. I shrank away.

" What's the difference between this little ol' paw and ya own?"

"It's black," I whimpered.

"That's true. Anything else?"

"It's bigger."

"Sure thing. Anything else?"

"D - D - Don't think so."

"Count the toes on your right front paw."

I quickly did as I was told. "Four."

"Yup four, that's normal for a cat. Now count mine."

"Seven?" I said, hardly believing I had counted correctly.

"Yup, seven," said Vince, with menace creeping into his voice. "Seven toes on each of ma front paws, and above each toe, what have I got?"

With a multiple, overlapping click, seven claws were unsheathed.

"Claws," I whispered.

"That's right, Little Buddy. With these I can cause a lot a damage - and ah don't mean collateral - git ma drift?"

"Yes sir!" I decided it would be wise to recognize Vince's superior fire power.

Vince hauled himself up onto my branch, and the claws retracted.

"Good. Now, I'll lay out the ground rules. First rule - ya call me Vince."

Vince was an American boxing cat, although he preferred to be known as a Hemingway, on account of some of his kin having lived with that great author. Vince ruled the gardens, and dealt ruthlessly with any cat brave or stupid enough to challenge him. As long as I stayed in my garden and only ventured out on his say so, we would get along fine. On that first short meeting, he gave me an excellent piece of advice, the first of many.

"If ya high tail it home now, Little Buddy, and push ya self through that cat flap, ya folks'll be so pleased to see ya, they'll forgive ya for running. And, there's another upside. Knowing you've gotten the hang of using it, you'll be free to come and go as ya please - from this day on."

I was doubtful, mainly because to do that I had to get past that enormous paw. He looked straight at me, gave what could possibly pass as a smile and winked one of his ghastly yellow eyes.

"Now, git!"

The bough shook as he jumped to the ground on his side of the wall. As he landed, I 'high tailed' - for my very own cat flap.

Vince was right. As soon as Jessica and Toby knew I had mastered the art of getting back through the cat flap, all travel restrictions were off, and the damage to Toby's hands forgotten. Well at least, by Jessica.

*****

"Are you evil, Vince?" Vince looked up at me for a long time before replying.

"Now that's one hell of a question, Little Buddy." He licked the back of an enormous paw and rubbed it over a bloated cheek. "Ya see, most cats are born killers, it's in our nature, and I guess I kill more than most. But that don't necessarily make me evil - least ah don't think so."

Vince was stretched out along the top of the garden wall. I was in the apple tree. It had become our regular meeting place. He paused, mid lick.

"Guess some folks think I'm evil. The daughter of my house refers to me as 'The Prince of Darkness', but I reckon that's cos I go out at night and there's always something dead laid out by the back door in the morning."

"I've killed a spider," I said, "Jessica was pleased about that, but when I killed a bird, she called me evil."

Vince laughed. "Humans are funny folk, Little Buddy. They even like dawgs. Come on, let me show ya something."

He rolled lazily off the wall, yet somehow managed an athletic landing on his lawn. I hesitated.

"It's okay Little Buddy, ya have ma permission."

I jumped down and followed him through the gardens; a route I had often seen him take when watching from the bedroom window.

Eventually, we arrived at a big house with a brick wall surrounding the garden. Without pause,Vince climbed a tree, walked along the top of a fence, jumped onto a shed roof and dropped down onto the wall. Having grown considerably since our first meeting, I followed every move with ease.

"This is Bloomfield House." Vince whispered, "It's owned by the Baines family. The original owners sold the land which all the others are built on, that's why it's gotta humdinger of a garden. Stay here and I'll see if the critter's at home."

I waited as instructed. Vince had taken us to a place on the wall, hidden from the house by a dense, evergreen shrub. He crept along the wall and peered through the outer fringe for several seconds before grunting with satisfaction.

"Yup, he's there. Ever seen a dawg before?"

"I've seen one on television - oh, and there were puppies in the pet shop."

"Well, now you're gonna see one in the flesh. It's dead asleep - and he's supposed to be a guard dawg! Let's have some fun."

Vince broke cover and we walked along the wall to sit down in full view of a large detached house with a long well kept lawn. Sun light glinted on the calm surface of a fish pond just below us. I was immediately drawn to it.

"Now pay attention, Little Buddy," chided Vince. "Fish ain't something ya need to know about, least ways, not today." He pointed a paw towards the house. "See the dawg sleeping on them steps?"

"The brown thing?"

"Yup. That's Benton. Benton's an Alsatian and although he don't look it from this distance, he's about the biggest Alsatian ya could git. Mr Baines thinks he's ferocious, so keeps him t' bark at the postman and t' keep cats outta the garden. Mr Baines hates cats, but likes getting letters."

He noticed my puzzled look and laughed, "Don't ask me, Little Buddy, I told ya, humans are funny." He pointed a paw towards the dog. "But, that's the challenge. Benton's there t' keep us out - so we're going in! "

Vince jumped down from the wall, a gigantic right paw missing the edge of the fish pond by a fraction. I followed, and as we sauntered side by side up the lawn towards Benton, Vince told me what to do.

"I'm gonna stop by this rose bed and rest awhile. You walk on up to the house and wake Benton. Suggest ya yell at him from about the length of ten cats – t' give ya self a good start - cos he will come at ya! When he does, run past me t' the fish pond, then turn, 'watch and learn'. Understand?"

"Yes, but what about you?"

"Just do as I say Little Buddy, then 'watch and learn'. Now git!"

Vince stretched out nonchalantly on the lawn by the round rose bed, exposing his soft underbelly. Heart pounding, I marched towards Benton. I knew I was getting bigger and faster by the week; trouble was, I had no idea how fast an Alsatian would be.

I mewed loudly as I approached, but Benton was in a deep sleep. I stopped at what I thought would be the right distance and made, what I considered to be one hell of a racket; but Benton slept on. My safety margin was down to about five cats, when an eye flicked open.

Initially a look of disbelief crossed Benton's face. He growled and grumbled. Then, his top lip curled and snarling loudly, he scrambled to his feet.

I turned and ran as if my life depended upon it, and at that time I really thought it did.

As I sped between Vince and the rose bed, he rolled over to face Benton. I heard a strangled squeal and turned to see if he needed help. A stupid thought! The growling, snarling dog had turned into a gibbering, whimpering wreck. It turned to run away, but with a flying leap, Vince was on his back, seven lethal claws slashing at each ear.

Benton desperately tried to shake him off as he ran yelping for the patio, but with claws sunk deep in dog flesh, Vince rode him with ease. When Benton reached the bottom of the steps, Vince boxed him viciously about the ears - one more time, just for luck - before dismounting and sauntering back towards me.

"There ya are, Little Buddy. Lesson one. Never turn ya back on a dawg."

"But you've just turned your back on him, Vince."

"Sure thing, but he won't chase me cos I've got - REPUTATION! And that's what we're gonna git for you, Little Buddy - REPUTATION. Now, pick a spot in the vegetable garden, it's the best place t' leave a calling card. Heh, heh, I just lurve it when poor old Benton gits inta trouble."

As we made our way back home, I questioned Vince again about being evil, but he dismissed the idea. He reckoned that if he was evil, he would have taken at least one of Benton's eyes out!

*****

The following day, we met under the hedge between our front gardens. Vince arranged the meeting under the pretext of warning me about the danger involved in crossing roads. Lesson number two, he called it.

"Folks living in your place before had a white fluffy cat called, Snowball. Real character Snowy, but his undoing was his aurophobia. His folks didn't recognize it in him. They laughed when Snowy ran sideways down the lawn, but when he ran sideways into the road, that was no laughing matter. Red bus - flat cat!"

"Why run sideways?"

"Aurophobic cats can't help it. Soon as the wind gits up, cats with aurophobia run sideways. They try to steer themselves straight with their tails, but it never works. They're skittish 'til they gits outta the wind. Shame about Snowy. Two more yards and he wudda made it to the bus shelter."

I looked at Vince in awe. "How do you know so much, Vince?"

"Ah, like I told ya, Little Buddy. 'Watch and learn'. Dawgs, like Benton can be trained, that's why humans like them so much. But when a dawg's asleep - it's asleep, and I mean - A SLEEP; it ain't learning nothing! But cats are different, we only pretend t' be asleep and if you're half-ways intelligent, that's when ya can learn - if ya has a mind to that is. My folks have got no idea that I know how to work their computer, and, if they caught me on it, they still wouldn't believe. But a dawg working the computer would be a different matter; they would believe and they would tell the world."

"That doesn't seem fair."

"Course it don't - it gives us cats a tremendous advantage and don't ya forget it. Invite me into your place sometime when your folks are out, Little Buddy and I'll give ya a computing lesson."

We both heard the footsteps, Vince gave me a nudge. "Ha, now this is what we've been waiting for - the postman."

We watched from under the hedge as the postman pushed letters through the letterbox at Vince's place. He said something about showing me how to greet a postmen, especially one wearing shorts, and told me to follow him, stand close and 'watch and learn'. The postman came through our gate holding a small package and a bundle of letters. He strode up the path to the front door and rang the door bell. That's when Vince crept out from under the hedge and I followed, not realizing he was about to attack!

Seven claws struck simultaneously behind each knee, sinking deep into exposed flesh. Then, simply by using his weight, he let them rake down, leaving long furrows which rapidly filled with blood. The postman let out a primeval howl of pain. I was rooted to the spot, watching as the blood ran down the back of his legs. He turned to see who or what had attacked him, but Vince had gone - he was under the hedge.

The front door opened and Jessica looked out. The postman pointed at me and turned to show Jessica the back of his legs. Jessica put a hand to her mouth in horror and, thanks to Vince, I gained my - REPUTATION!

CHAPTER THREE: THE BLAME GAME

When Jessica cleaned and applied antiseptic cream to the deep wounds on the back of the postman's legs, it should have been obvious from the number of scratches, that I was not the culprit.

Fortunately, common sense did not prevail and Toby and Jessica received a letter from the Post Office, warning that all deliveries would be suspended if they failed to control their ferocious cat.

When I told Vince he laughed so much, he almost fell off the wall. "Good one, Little Buddy. Now we have to work to enhance that reputation."

"Perhaps I should scratch the back of Toby's legs?"

Vince shook his head. "Bad idea; it won't spread the word outside your family and Toby could make life difficult. Let me sleep on it."

I left him in a fitful doze and went home. A worried Jessica had been calling me; it was almost post delivery time! The clunk of the cat flap brought her rushing into the kitchen from the front door, where she had been keeping an anxious look-out. I rubbed against her legs and purred. She picked me up.

"Thank goodness you're in Lettuce. You really must stop terrorizing the postman, he's had to stop wearing shorts. I don't know what came over you - we've had to warn all our friends."

So, the word was spreading; could Vince be wrong? Perhaps an attack on Toby would enhance my reputation after all? I heard the letter box rattle and a few seconds later, Toby came into the kitchen with a fan of letters.

"Hello tiger, how are you today?" He stretched out a hand and touched my nose with a finger, an affectionate gesture which he often used, but, I bit him! Not just a nip; my teeth went right down to the bone. He uttered an expletive and slapped my face with the letters. It was an admonishment, not intended to hurt, but Jessica turned to shield me from him.

"Stop it Toby! I won't have you attack a defenseless kitten."

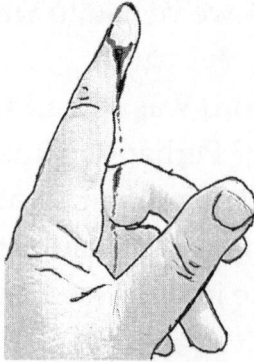

Toby held up his finger which was streaming blood. "A defenseless kitten? Since when was Lettuce defenseless? Look at the size of her - she's no longer a kitten Jess, she's a killer!"

To add weight to Toby's assessment, I made a dreadful growling sound which came from somewhere deep in my stomach, almost frightening myself in the process. I wriggled free from Jessica's loving arms and as I hurled myself at the cat flap, they began to argue, and for some inexplicable reason, I felt quite pleased with myself.

Time to kill a mouse!

Vince had shown me a garden where there was a nest of field mice, but pointed out that there would be no credit in catching one until they were of a size which would impress my folks.

Today could be that day. Not wishing to disturb Vince, I went over the fence on the other side of our garden and worked my way around.

It took a patient hour waiting in the long grass behind a garden shed, but eventually I had my prey.

With a fat field mouse, wriggling between my teeth, I hurried home to show Vince, but he was not on the wall. Disappointed I took the mouse into our garden and let it go in the middle of the lawn. It made a dash for freedom, but I pounced before it reached the flower border.

I repeated this several times, until tiring of the game, I threw the mouse high in the air, killing it with a crunching bite as I leapt and caught it three feet from the ground. I felt exhilarated by the kill, but it didn't last. I thought about eating the mouse, but changed my mind and laid it out carefully by the back door for Jessica.

The corner of the patio, where the garden wall abutted the house, was a glorious sun trap and a favorite place for a doze. I lay stretched out on my back, eyes half closed looking up through a sweet smelling trellis of honeysuckle. It had been a good morning. Toby's thumb, bitten to the bone; and my first mouse, killed and laid out for inspection. I settled in for a contented cat nap, but within a few minutes, sensed a presence on the wall above me.

"Pleased with ya self, Little Buddy?" I squinted through the honeysuckle, his yellow eyes were difficult to locate among the red and yellow flowers, but I knew he was up there somewhere. "Yup," I said, "my first mouse."

"Very laudable," replied Vince, "but I've got something that will do more for ya reputation than an itty bitty mouse."

Something dark and heavy thudded down onto the patio. It was a large, dead rat!

Vince followed it down, and showed me how to lay it out for best effect.

"There you are, Little Buddy. Now, down to business. Are your folks at home?"

"No, they're at work."

"Well, ain't that just dandy. If you was to invite me in, you could have your first computing lesson."

"Okay, Little Buddy. You're encrypted!"

Vince gave the keyboard a final tap with an extended single claw on his left paw. It was something he made me practice as he created my very own user account, having demonstrated how impossible it would be to tap a single key with a paw.

There was a lot to learn, but Vince assured me that if I watched Jessica and Toby when they were using the computer, I would soon be able to master it.

He winked and grinned. "They'll never suspect that ya have your own space on their computer."

Although I did not know it at the time, I was about to face my first winter and I would be devoting a large slice of my waking hours on a voyage to computer literacy!

CHAPTER FOUR: JOEY

I enjoyed the changing seasons. When the
wind blew and the leaves fell from the apple
tree, I remembered Vince's story about Snowy.
The wind had an affect on me; not to the same
extent, although I did enjoy running up the
garden with the wind in my tail.

My hiding place in the apple tree soon
disappeared and Vince and I met in sheltered
places, sometimes under his folks' car,
sometimes at the back of our garage, and often
indoors, when the coast was clear.

I experienced several sharp frosts,
which I quite enjoyed - it made my fur tingle.

But the first snow took me by surprise. I was in a hurry and jumped out through the cat flap into two inches of cold white stuff! I know it doesn't sound much, but to the uninitiated it came as quite a shock. I found some exposed earth under a shrub, did what I had to do, and rushed back indoors. Toby thought it very funny as I hurtled past him and made for the stairs.

Jessica had drawn the curtains back in their bedroom, so I surveyed the scene. Everything had turned white apart from Vince, who was walking along the top of the garden wall towards me. He indicated that I should join him outside, I really did not want to, but had my reputation to think of.

Vince was waiting as I emerged from the cat flap. I followed him down the garden and up into the apple tree, where he insisted I look back at our lawn.

"What d'ya see, Little Buddy."
I looked towards the house, wondering what it was he wanted me to see.

"No, in the snow. Those are our tracks."

"Ah, yes. I can see them now."

"That's right, Little Buddy. And if we can see them, so can other creatures. In last winter's snow, two cats disappeared, and d'ya know why?"

"Because they got lost?"

"Nope, they got taken by a fox. They were hiding and thought they were safe, but their tracks gave them away. So take care, Little Buddy. If you're out in the snow, watch ya back and if ya stop, climb high."

"I will, Vince. Thanks."

"That's OK – jist remember what ah told ya. Now; we'll have a little amble - see what's going on."

We had walked through a couple of gardens when it began to snow and before long it was what Vince called, a white out. I couldn't see anything, not even the hedge we had crawled though a few seconds before. Vince told me to stick close to his tail and led me back to our patio.

I found snow a bit scary, although I did not admit as much to Vince. I made the excuse that I needed more time on the computer and rarely ventured out in the snow during that first winter.

By the time the weather began to improve, I was regularly checking the emails received by Toby and Jessica and their online activity. Toby was feverishly looking for gifts and the like and it began to dawn on me that Jessica's birthday was fast approaching. Vince said that would figure because I was over a year old.

I was ready for the flood of birthday cards which arrived for Jessica, but not for Toby's present. I was grooming on the patio when he crept in through the side gate. He was carrying a large box shaped object covered in blue cloth, with a pink ribbon rosette on the top. He put a finger to his mouth to signify that I should keep quiet.. What was I likely to do, start a cat's chorus?

I watched him struggle through the back door, waited a few seconds, then went through my cat flap to investigate.

The box was on the kitchen table. Toby was on his way to fetch Jessica. I jumped up on the table, and seeing that the blue cloth was draped over and not wrapped around the box, lifted a corner with my computer claw to take a peek. It was a cage! Surely not another cat? I sniffed and got a distinct acidic smell; definitely not feline! I lifted the cloth higher.

"Squawk! It's the cat! Poor Joey - it's the cat!"

A bright blue bird furiously flapped its wings before retreating to the far side of the cage. Taken by surprise, I jumped down from the table forgetting to disengage my claw. The cloth was attached to the top of the cage where the pink rosette was tied and the cage followed me down to the floor with an almighty crash.

Not waiting to check if the blue bird had survived the fall, I unhooked my claw and legged it through the cat flap.

"Seems to me they've gotten themselves a budgerigar. They'll call it a budgie, though strictly speaking it's a melopsittacus indulatus." Vince savored the Latin name, pausing for effect before asking. "Are ya sure they're blaming you for the accident, Little Buddy?"

"Very sure: I heard them arguing. Jessica suggested Toby must have put the cage too close to the edge of the table. Toby said he definitely placed it in the middle. The bird told him it was the cat and he heard me go out through my flap."

"That's the trouble with cat flaps, darn noisy. Only way is to let the flap drop down onto ya tail, then pull through until it slips off the end. Makes for a silent entrance - or exit."

"Is that how your tail got bent?"

Vince looked at his bent tail and gave me a rueful smile. "Nope. That was a dawg."

"Benton?"

"No, long before Benton. I'll tell ya the story sometime, but for now, we've got that pesky budgerigar to worry about. Could be that the only words it knows is its own name, and 'It's the cat'. That alone could be enough t' git ya blamed for everything that goes wrong in ya household. But, if it's got a wider vocabulary, that noisy little critter could become an informer! You've gotta take action, and fast, Little Buddy. I suggest ya go back through that cat flap, using my silent entry method, and find out what's going on."

As I crept towards the half open living room door, I could hear the bird going through its repertoire, much to the delight and amusement of Jessica. Vince was right, the pesky bird could become an informer. Had Toby bought him to spy on me? Even as I listened he was encouraging the bird to do just that.

"Where's that cat Joey? Where's that cat?"

Joey flapped his wings and squawked. "It's the cat! it's the cat!"

"We know it was the cat, Joey, but what did she do to your cage?"

Joey looked at Toby, then into a small round mirror. "Pretty boy Joey."

I began to wonder if the budgerigar had any idea what it was saying, or why. I sauntered into the room and jumped onto Jessica's lap

"It's the Cat! It's the cat!"

I stopped wondering. Vince was right. The noisy little budgerigar did have the potential to become an informer! Joey had to go, but how?

My arrival on Jessica's lap not only set Joey off, it reignited the argument over why the budgie cage crashed to the floor. Jessica was firmly on my side, it was obvious to her that Toby could not have heard me going out through the cat flap as I had been in the house all the time. Toby said he saw me on the patio when he brought Joey in through the back door. Jessica said he was either mistaken, or her darling Lettuce must have followed him in through the back door at the same time. As the argument raged, I closed my eyes. To Toby it looked as if I was asleep, which did nothing to improve his temper; he wanted to ban me from the sitting room. Jessica emphatically said no, and pointed out that the cage was suspended from a stand, which was cat proof, and anyway, I would never be able to open the cage door.

If she had known about my computer claw, she may have thought differently. A plan was forming in my devious mind, a plan which would see the back of Joey yet attach no blame to me.

To put the plan into operation, all I had to do was wait patiently for favorable conditions - a combination of Jessica and Toby at work and a small window, above the large window looking out over the patio and garden, left open.

Eventually, my patience was rewarded, and as Jessica and Toby drove off, I climbed onto the back of the armchair close to Joey's cage and spoke to him.

"Hi Joey, how would you like to escape to freedom?"

He looked at me, head cocked to one side, listening. Perhaps he was smarter than I thought?

"Look through the window, Joey. That's the garden and it leads to other gardens and most have trees. You'll have a wonderful time out there, flying from tree to tree."

He chattered excitedly and moved along his perch towards me. It looked as if he was up for it.

"I'm going to open the cage door. I won't harm you, that's a promise. I'll move aside and let you fly to freedom through the open window."

I pointed towards the small open window. Joey chattered and nodded his head up and down, in what I interpreted as understanding. As I reached out and hooked my computer claw in the door catch, he exercised his wings. The door opened easily enough. I gave it a push to help it swing wide open and retreated to the chair back as promised.

With no hesitation, Joey flew out from his cage . He completed two circuits of the room close to the ceiling, before leveling out to fly at speed towards freedom. I shouted to remind him. "Small window, Joey! Small window !" But Joey maintained his course and flew full tilt into the large window with a solid thud. Wings fluttering he slid down behind a framed photograph on the window sill, of Jessica and Toby cutting the cake on their wedding day. Taking great care not to disturb any of the ornaments, especially the prized photograph, I jumped up to check on him. He was out cold, so I decided the best place for him to recover, would be in the garden.

I carried Joey gingerly through my cat flap, not wanting to bite into his tiny body and gently laid him out on the patio, then stood guard, waiting for him to recover.

Looking around, I can honestly say I thought Joey would not be disappointed when he regained consciousness. Apart from my apple tree, which was a favorite place for songbirds, there was a cherry tree, close to the fence on the opposite side of the garden. In the garden backing onto ours, there was an evergreen of some description, a plum and another apple tree.

"You really will enjoy yourself out here, Joey," I said, looking down at his prone body. I gave him a push with my paw, thinking that might help wake him up. He rolled over, head lolling to one side. I pushed him back and it lolled over to the other side, then it dawned on me. Joey was dead! Not only that, his body was laid out where all my kills were exhibited as trophies for Jessica!

The main thing I learned that day is that cats and budgies do not communicate and budgies only repeat what humans say to them, without any understanding. Joey could not have become an informer even if he had lived to a ripe old age!

As it was, he was a dead budgerigar and I had to dispose of his body. Time was on my side, so I sat and thought it through. My original plan still held good. With the cage door open and the small window propped open, Jessica and Toby would assume the door to the cage had not been closed properly and Joey had escaped into the garden. I could hide his body somewhere in our garden, but Jessica and Toby would make a thorough search, and if they found the body, I could still be the natural culprit. The same held good if I hid it in a neighbor's garden; except for one! I picked Joey up in my mouth, not so gently this time, and carried him down the lawn.

From my apple tree, a careful appraisal of Vince's house and garden ascertained that Mrs Jenks was at home, and Vince was inside, probably having his customary nap following a night on the prowl. I jumped to the ground, and keeping close to the wall, made my way through the densely planted border, to their patio. The television was on in the living room. I could see Mrs Jenks watching from her favorite armchair. I moved closer to the house, narrowing the angle to a point where she would not be able to see me. Praying she would not come to the kitchen, I crept over to the place where Vince laid out his kills. I was tempted to drop Joey and run, but knowing how Vince operated, I laid Joey out precisely, just as he would have done. At last, satisfied with my work, I returned to the cover of the border and sneaked home.

Jessica was upset when she discovered that Joey had escaped from his cage. She was in the garden calling for him when the door bell rang. Toby opened the door. I was pretending to be asleep on the fourth step of the stairs, a favorite place which gave me a view through to the hall one way and the kitchen in the other. Mr and Mrs Jenks stood in the doorway. Mrs Jenks was holding Joey's body, wrapped in a canary yellow silk handkerchief, a little inappropriate I thought, given the sadness of the occasion. She said she was very sorry and was about to hand the small bundle to Toby when Jessica rushed in from the kitchen, so she handed it to her instead.

"We are so sorry," said Mr Jenks, "but I'm afraid Vince has killed your budgerigar."

Jessica sobbed as she peeled back a corner of the yellow silk handkerchief to look at Joey's body. She gave her neighbors a brave smile.

"It's not your fault, and we can't blame Vince for being a cat. If Toby had closed the cage door properly, this would never have happened!"

Setting Jessica against Toby had not been part of the plan, which was a shame, because had it been, it was beginning to work perfectly!

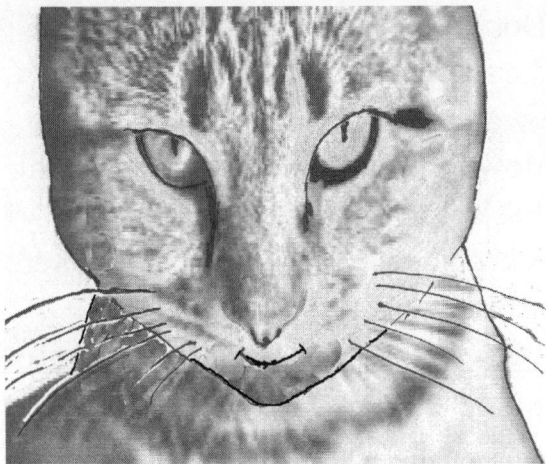

Joey was buried in the garden, wrapped in the silk handkerchief, which Mrs Jenks insisted should be used for the purpose. I watched the ceremony from the bedroom window.

Vince was watching from the garden wall, under the apple tree. I thought he would be impressed with the way I dealt with the Joey situation and could hardly wait to explain how I worked everything out. I waited until Jessica and Toby came back in before running down the garden.

I announced my arrival as I walked along the bough to my usual place in the apple tree. "Hi Vince."

"Don't 'Hi Vince' me, ya two timing tabby," he snarled.

It was not the greeting I expected. I looked down through the leaves to see him staring back at me. The ghastly yellow malevolence filled eyes were back and there was no friendly smile of welcome.

"You've crossed the line and as from now, you're ma sworn enemy. Set as much as one paw in ma territory, and you will be one dead cat."

"But Vince," I protested, "I thought you'd take it as a joke."

"Take an affront to ma hunting prowess as a joke? You've got the wrong guy. You've damaged ma reputation, I don't go around killing pet budgerigars. Now git, before ah really lose ma temper and take a swipe at ya!"

He backed up the threat by raising one of his enormous paws with all seven claws extended. I didn't hang around to argue.

CHAPTER FIVE: A CLOSE ENCOUNTER.

Life without a regular laugh and chat with Vince was boring. I filled my time honing my computer skills and watching day time television. This was driving Toby to distraction because he meticulously turned off the TV before going to work, but found it on when he came home!

One afternoon, as I was surfing the channels, I came across a fishing program. I know fishing can be boring to some, but not to a cat. Like an angler, we are extremely patient in pursuit of our prey.

I was delighted when a tasty looking fish was reeled in, but less so when the angler carefully took it off the hook - and let it go! Where was the sense in that?

"Keep it! Eat it!" I shouted at the screen, but to no avail.

After releasing his catch, the angler spoke about different lures and hooks. Of course, I knew I would never be able to lay my paws on those, but there was one thing I did have. I flicked out my computer claw. That would make as good a fishing hook as any I had seen.

That night, I went fishing!

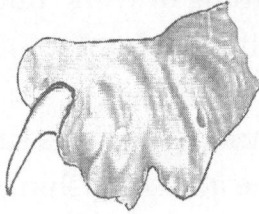

Since my falling out with Vince, I had adopted a new route through the gardens. It intersected with his at a couple of points, so not wishing to get on the wrong end of those enormous paws, I proceeded with great caution. My objective? The fish pond at Benton's place.

Eventually, I was on top of the wall, peering through the outer fringe of the evergreen shrub. All lights were out in the big house and there was no sign of Benton, I guessed he would have guard duties indoors.

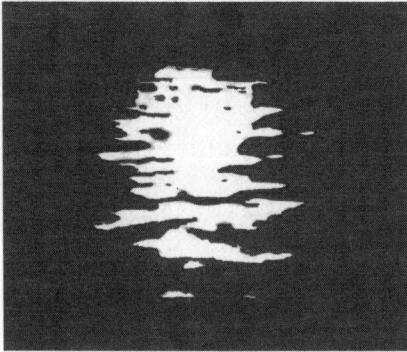

The moon was reflected in the smooth black surface of the pond. How many fish were hiding in those inky depths? Would they be too deep for me to reach?

A ripple traveled cross the surface, and a white shape appeared at the far edge of the pond - it was a large fish! It nudged into the fringe, setting off another series of ripples. It was feeding and amazingly, with the garden so silent and still, I could hear it munching.

I crept along the wall and jumped down onto the soft earth of a flowerbed, well away from the pond, but as I approached, the fish backed away from the fringe and sank into the depths.

Sitting back from the edge, I studied the pond for sometime before reaching the conclusion that if the fish had found something to feed on in the fringe beneath me, it could return to the same position. I laid low and waited.

Eventually my patience was rewarded. The fish rose silently to the surface, drifted towards me and began to feed as its nose touched the fringe. I let it feed for several minutes before slowly lowering my paw into the water under its belly.

Then, with one swift movement, I drove my hook claw in and scooped upwards. The fish wriggled off my claw, but not before I had it on the bank where it thrashed around, jumping back towards the pond. I scooped it up again, throwing it further up the bank. The fish tried another couple of jumps then subsided, gasping.

It was a large fish, as long as me without my tail. How was I going to get it home? I was so intent on solving the problem, the fox took me by surprise.

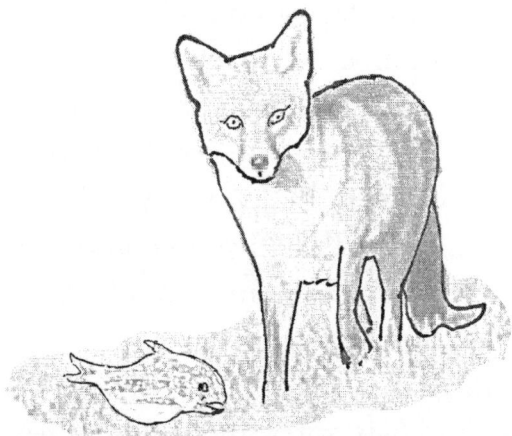

Suddenly he was there! I backed away, reluctantly leaving my catch for him. He looked at me and licked his lips.

This was the fox Vince had warned me about. He called him Reynard, because that, he said, was the common name for all male foxes. I joked and said that if I shouted Reynard, would several foxes pop their heads up? He fixed me with those yellow eyes of his and told me not to joke about it. Reynard was a killer and responsible for the disappearance of more cats than the two he had mentioned.

Reynard sniffed at the fish, then smirked as he stepped daintily around it. He had me cornered! My back was against the wall and he could cut-off any move I made to the right. To the left, the pond was flush with the wall. If I went that way, I would have to swim for it. I had no idea if I could swim, but was pretty sure that a fox would be well versed in that sort of thing.

Reynard crept closer. "My cubs prefer red meat to fish, sorry about that," he said silkily. "You can't get away. If you give up without a fight I will make your death as quick and painless as possible."

I glared back at him. "I'll take your eyes out Reynard, I suggest you take the fish and avoid a lot of pain." I did not feel as brave as I was trying to sound.

Reynard sneered. "No cat has ever got the better of me, and I don't see a flabby tabby succeeding where others have failed. You will make a good meal for my cubs, so prepare to die."

I tensed my back legs ready to spring. My claws were unsheathed. I would go straight for those mocking eyes.

Reynard lunged towards me, confident in his superiority. I took a swipe at his nose and drew first blood. Enraged he opened his jaws and snapped, narrowly missing my face. I swiped at his eyes with both paws, but he swayed away, laughing. "Die tabby - die."

Suddenly, something black, hissing, spitting and screaming, crashed through the evergreen shrub and landed on Reynard's back. It was Vince!

Reynard was taken completely by surprise as fourteen claws dug deep. dragging his head away from me.

"Git, Little Buddy, git!"

I was tempted to run, but there was still the question of the fish. Vince seemed to read my mind as Reynard wailed and tried to turn his head to attack the devil on his back.

"Forget the fish! Git! I can't hold him forever!"

I really was about to go, but the fox squirmed, turned and sank its teeth into Vince's leg. He chewed on it and Vince howled in agony. But Reynard's throat was exposed! I hurled myself at him and burrowing my head into thick fur, bit deep into his throat, gnawing and tearing.

The fox let go of Vince's leg and tried to attack me.

I spat and yowled; the noise from the three of us was enough to waken the dead. There was a shout from the big house and outside lights came on.

"Kill, Benton! Kill!"

Benton charged down the garden. Vince rolled off the back of Reynard as Benton's jaws clamped around his neck. He lifted Reynard's body and shook it vigorously from side to side, before dropping it to the ground.

"Kill those cats, Benton! Kill them! Kill them!"

A bright beam from a torch swept the garden – searching - searching.

Benton looked at Vince who was dragging his savaged leg. "Hide," he said. "I won't give you away."

"Yeah. You expect us to believe that," I said.

"I do," said Vince. "Come on , Little Buddy, under the evergreen. "Thanks Benton."

Mr Baines arrived on the scene to find Benton standing guard over the dead fox. The beam from his torch found the big fish and he gasped in horror.

"My prize carp!" Falling to his knees, he picked it up and cradling it in his arms, took it back to the pond and held it under water.

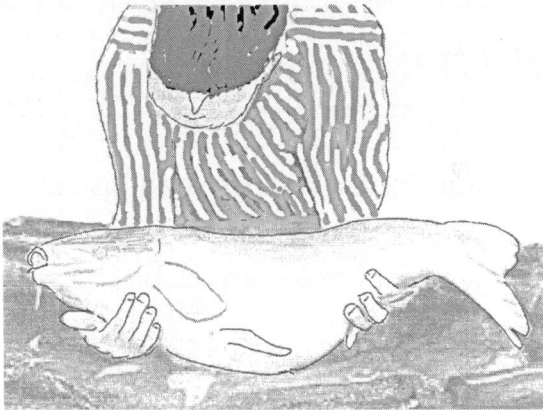

The carp stirred back to life. Mr Baines grunted his satisfaction and let it swim away.

"Good boy, Benton. What happened to the cats?"

Benton went to the other side of the pond and stretched his front legs up against the wall.

"Over there, huh? I'm going to get some razor wire to go along the top of the wall - let them try climbing over that!"

Satisfied with the severity of his threat, he patted Benton on the head. "Good boy, you scared off the cats and killed the fox."

"No, he didn't," I whispered indignantly to Vince, "we did."

"Makes no difference," Vince whispered back."The fox is dead: now button that lip."

Mr Baines made Benton pose by Reynard and took a picture with his cell phone. The flash lit up our hiding place and I thought he must have seen us, but he was admiring the picture.

" I reckon this could make the front page of the local paper," he chuckled, "maybe the nationals, or even television."

Satisfied, he walked, or perhaps I should say, waddled, because he was massively overweight, back to the house. Benton made a detour to tell us to wait until they were in the house, before breaking cover.

"Is he letting us go so that he can get all the credit for killing Reynard?"

Vince grunted. "He would've got the credit anyway. He let us go out of respect, Little Buddy."

I felt a pang of guilt. "Thanks for coming to my rescue Vince. How did you know the fox was about?"

"Saw him trailing ya, so I trailed him."

"Sorry about your leg."

"Not your fault Little Buddy. Come on, let's git."

With his damaged leg, Vince could not jump and had to use those powerful front paws to drag himself up through the shrub and onto the wall. He limped along the top, leaving a trail of blood. There was a lot of it and I began to worry that he might not make it home. Vince was used to jumping and climbing and without the full use of his back legs, it would be impossible to follow his normal route.

Since our falling out, my way through the gardens favored wriggling under fences and crawling through hedges. I led the way and Vince was happy to follow. It was slow progress, but at long last he hauled himself through a hole at the bottom of our garden and collapsed on the lawn.

I ran for help, and made a hell of a racket as I burst through the cat flap. Jessica and Toby were in bed, which was no great surprise, as the kitchen clock showed just after 3am. I ran up the stairs meowing loudly. Toby turned on his bedside light as I pushed open the bedroom door.

"What the hell's going on, Lettuce?"

Jessica sat up and shrieked. "She's covered in blood!"

Toby got out of bed. I turned tail and ran back down the stairs, meowing. I heard Toby cursing and Jessica getting out of bed. They were taking too long! I ran back up the stairs and howled at them through the open door. Jessica was putting on her dressing gown. She was truly shocked by my appearance and what she interpreted as a howl of pain.

"Call the vet, Toby! Lettuce is badly hurt!"

"Not bad enough to stop her running up and down the stairs," commented Toby, as I scampered back down. "I don't want to get a vet out on a wild goose chase, and anyway, how am I going to get one at this time in the morning?"

"Just do it, Toby, Lettuce needs help."

When Jessica came into the kitchen, I was waiting by the cat flap. She switched on the lights, which were a series of spotlights in the ceiling and one was pointing directly at me. Covered with Reynard's blood, I must have looked dreadful so I can understand why she thought I was badly injured. She moved towards me and crouched down.

"Come here Lettuce darling. Let me see where you're hurt."

I gave her the little "purp" I used to let her know I was pleased to see her, hoping somehow it would tell her I was okay and it was Vince who needed her help.

As she stretched a hand towards me, I gave another "purp", turned and went out through the cat flap.

Jessica was quick on the uptake. When she opened the door, and shone the torch on me. I raised my tail and using it as a flag, led her down the garden to Vince, who managed to lift his head and give her a soft mew of welcome.

"Oh, Vince! What have you done?"

I wanted to tell her it was the fox, but Jessica was already on the case.

"I don't think you got that fighting another cat - can I take a look?"

Vince said it was no problem, but of course Jessica only heard it as a meow, and proceeded with caution. She shuddered when she saw the extent of the damage, but managed a smile as she stroked Vince on the head.

"Don't worry Vince, help is on the way. Toby has called for the vet."

Toby came out to join us.

"Did you get one?"

"They're opening up for us, but we will have to take Lettuce to the surgery."

"It's not Lettuce, it's Vince. His back right leg is in a terrible mess. Looks as if a dog's been chewing on it. I'll stay with him, you go and tell Walter and Helen.

By the time Mr and Mrs Jenks arrived on the scene, Jessica had checked me out and couldn't believe I had no injury. Where had all the blood come from? It was caked on my face, paws and chest.

She tried cleaning it off with kitchen wipes, but I was having none of that and scrambled away.

Vince was wrapped in a sheet and carried by Mr Jenks to their car, where he laid him on a blanket on the back seat.

"See ya, Little Buddy." Vince winked a yellow eye.

"It will be alright, Vince," said Mrs Jenks soothingly, thinking he was complaining about his leg.

As they drove off, Jessica said, "I do hope the vet can patch him up."

"Looked bad," said Toby. "Probably best to have him put to sleep."

At that moment, I realized my dislike of Toby had turned to hatred

CHAPTER SIX: THE BLAME GAME.

It was mid morning by the time Mr and Mrs Jenks returned. I was waiting under the front hedge as their car turned in off the road. I walked over and brushed against Mr Jenks as he stepped out of the car. He looked down at me and tried to smile. "Hello, Lettuce. If you're looking for Vince I'm afraid you're going to be disappointed." He sighed and stroked my head. "Don't know what you two were up to, but his injuries were horrendous." He reached into the car, picked up the sheet and blanket Vince had been wrapped in, and walked slowly to their back door. Mrs Jenks said nothing. She wouldn't even look at me. I think she thought I was responsible for what had happened to Vince, and in a way, I suppose I was.

The killing of the fox was reported in 'The Echo', the local weekly newspaper, which had long been campaigning against 'The Urban Fox'. The picture taken by Mr Baines, with Benton standing over poor old Reynard, made the front page. Benton saved the prize carp for his master and made the neighborhood a safer place for cats. No connection was made between Vince, me and the fox, but someone must have heard us fighting.

Days went by and I was desperate for news. Did Mr and Mrs Jenks take Toby's advice and have Vince put to sleep? I tried everything, even resorted to using Vince's silent method of entry to sneak through his cat flap and eavesdrop on conversations between Mr and Mrs Jenks. All to no avail, they were very glum and a brief conversation over vet fees, was the closest they came to discussing Vince.

Then, I had a breakthrough, which came from an unexpected source.

"You've got a nerve, coming back here."
I looked down from the Baines' garden wall.

"What's with not barking, Benton? You should give a defenseless cat fair warning."

He looked at me with what in a dog's world would possibly pass as a wry smile. "Defenseless cat? You and Vince were ripping that fox to pieces. I almost felt sorry for it."

"Huh, you might, but I don't. Reynard gnawed Vince's leg and he's been taken to the vet to be put to sleep."

"Well now," said Benton, "it seems I might have some news for you, but move along the wall out of sight of the house, I'm in enough trouble as it is."

I shuffled back into the cover of the evergreen shrub. Benton moved closer, pretending to sniff around the edge of the pond.

"What news?" I asked eagerly.

"Did you see the piece in The Echo?"

"Where they portrayed you as the cats' hero? That's old news - and not true - as you well know."

Benton shrugged. "Ah, well, I had no choice, not if I wanted to give you and Vince time to escape. But it all backfired on me, I'm no longer the hero, but that's only part of the news." Benton went on to tell me that a junior reporter from The Echo, visited them for a follow-up story. Mr Baines, was only too pleased to co-operate, hoping the story would go national. The reporter said she hoped so too, and took photographs of Benton in various poses by the fish pond, and the place where Reynard died. But, when she loaded the photographs into the 'Dead Fox File' back at the office, she noticed something which had been missed in the original picture sent in by Mr Baines.

The editor had cropped in tight on the subject for the newspaper article, but on the original, in the dark area behind Benton, there were four pin points of light. She zoomed in, fiddled with picture adjustments - and - there we were, two cats hiding under a bush, the flash from the camera reflected in our eyes.

The junior reporter felt she was onto something and her working title for the follow-up story was - "KILLER CATS!"

Mr Baines was furious - Benton would have to go! Moira, the reporter, had spoken with the RSPCA who confirmed that although a broken neck was the cause of Reynard's death, there were deep wounds to the back of the head and his ears had been torn to shreds; consistent with an attack by a very large cat. His throat had been torn open, but the wound was too small to have been inflicted by a dog. Inquiries at the town veterinary practice revealed that a large black cat was recovering from severe leg wounds in their animal hospital. They had suggested putting him to sleep, but his owners insisted that everything possible should be done to save him.

I thanked Benton for the good news, and wished him well. On my way back through the gardens - I wondered if Mr Baines would have Benton put to sleep - gave three silent cheers for Mr and Mrs Jenks - and vowed to give Toby a good scratching!

*****

I was loitering under the front hedge as the Jenks car pulled into their drive. Mrs Jenks opened the back door and Vince's face, framed by what looked like a lamp shade, peered out.

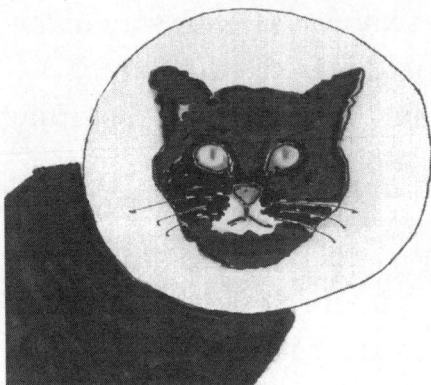

He saw me and growled. "Any comments about this contraption, Little Buddy and you'll be back on ma black list."

"Good to see you, Vince, but what's it for?"

"T' stop me gnawing at ma own leg, as if that's likely to happen. I'd leave that to a pesky fox."

Shrugging off any help from Mrs Jenks, Vince eased himself out of the car and limped over to me. His damaged leg was heavily bandaged.

"So, what's the news?"

"I was interested in that fish, so I went over to Benton's place."

Vince smirked. "You've got a nerve."

"That's what Benton said, but he's in trouble. Mr Baines knows he let us stay in the garden after Reynard was killed. Moira, a junior reporter from the newspaper, is writing a follow-up story about killer cats."

The lampshade moved slowly from side to side before Vince added gravely. "Benton's not in trouble - he's in deep do dah! Mr Baines will view saving us as a betrayal. He won't want him anymore and my guess is he would rather have Benton put down than find a new home for him!"

"I was thinking that he might have him put to sleep. That's what Toby thought they should have done to you."

"Did he now? Well, I'll tell ya something' for nothing'. Being put to sleep is the same as being put down - jist sounds better. Once I'm fit again, I'll get ma own back on Toby!"

"I've already done it," I said proudly. "I gave him a severe scratching."

Vince grinned at me through his tunnel. "Nice one, Little Buddy. I'm glad you've taken the initiative, cos I'm gonna have to rely on ya t' save Benton."

"How can I do that?"

"That's for you t' figure out. I'll be outta action for a while, so git!"

I watched Vince limp towards Mrs Jenks who had been calling him. Her look told me she still held me responsible.

CHAPTER SEVEN: AN EXOTIC SOLUTION.

I met Ting Ling on the fence at the bottom of her garden, which adjoined the wall about halfway down the Baines property. Her folks were their next door neighbors. If Ting Ling was surprised to see me she did not show it.

"I was half expecting you - yet not expecting," she said in a sing song voice as she walked along the narrow top of the fence towards me. She was a Siamese and although we nodded on passing, had never had a conversation. She walked delicately and precisely, her tail held high with the tip flicking from side to side for balance, but the tail was so slender, I could hardly believe it would make any difference.

She sat down at a safe distance and looked at me; or rather, past me. Her left eye seemed to be looking over my left shoulder and her right eye over my right. Very strange!

"Hi Ting Ling, wonder if you know what's happening to Benton?"

Ting Ling tilted her head. "I see everything - yet I see nothing."

"We heard Mr Baines is going to get rid of Benton."

"I hear everything - yet I hear nothing."

"Word is, he's going to have him put down!"

"I know everything - yet I know nothing."

Vince had warned me that Ting Ling spoke in riddles and I would have to be patient, but with her silly nonsense and supercilious smirk, it was all I could do to resist giving her a swipe across the nose. But I was desperate to know about Benton so I gave her one of my best smiles.

"If you knew Benton was going to be put down, you would let me know?"

She sniffed and squinted. "Why would cat help dog - yet why wouldn't cat help dog?"

I eased along the fence to get her in range. She deserved a jolly good swipe. She moved back a corresponding distance.

"Benton going to vet tomorrow - yet, he may not go to vet tomorrow."

I snapped."He's either going or he's not! Now, which is it?" I raised a threatening paw, but she smiled her infuriating, superior smile.

"It is for you to decide - or not decide." She turned and sauntered away, pausing to look over her shoulder. "Mr Baines very impatient - yet could become patient."

Now what did she mean by that? It was too late to ask, Ting Ling had jumped down into her own garden and vanished into the shrubbery.

I turned and walked along the narrow fence to the Baines wall. It was only a small jump onto the wall, but as far as I could see, I would be in full view of the house until I could get to a group of golden juniper, their feathery tops peeping over the wall. It wouldn't be much in the way of cover, but if I kept low it should do. I took the risk and moved quickly into position.

There was no activity at the back of the house. Benton was nowhere to be seen. Had Mr Baines already carried out his dastardly threat? I crept along the wall to my next point of cover - the garage. It was long and high with eaves hanging over the wall and a pathway which ran from the front of the house to the back garden. I moved quickly along this corridor of excellent cover, making a mental note of any escape routes along the way. A plum tree in Ting Ling's garden was well within leaping distance.

I heard someone calling out and approached the end of the garage with caution.

Mr Baines was cleaning his large 4x4. Vince once told me that humans looked like their cars. I laughed at what he obviously meant as a joke, but in Mr Baines case, with his large stomach swaying from side to side as he polished, there was a definite similarity

"Telephone for you, Desmond. It's Moira." I recognized the voice. It was Mrs Baines.

"I don't know a Moira."

"Yes you do, it's Moira, the reporter from The Echo."

"Oh that Moira. Tell her I've got nothing to add to her story."

"It's not her story, it's Benton. She wants to buy him. She doesn't want him to be put to sleep."

Mr Baines furiously polished a shiny strip of aluminum. "Tell her to mind her own business. Benton will be put down tomorrow and that's that. He's no use as a guard dog and he's no use to me. He let me down!"

"But she would give him a good home."
The plaintive tone in Mrs Baines' voice
encouraged me to edge forward. She was
leaning out through the front door, holding a
telephone with a hand over the mouthpiece.
Despite being in slippers and a dressing gown,
she came out onto the steps, obviously
concerned about Benton. Mr Baines threw the
polishing cloth down in a fit of rage.

"Enough, Sylvia!" he shouted. "Benton's
going to be put down tomorrow and that's an
end to it!"

Angrily, he opened the car, got in,
slammed the door, started the engine and the
big car lurched towards the gates. I thought he
was going to crash into them, but the car
screeched to a halt and he impatiently revved
the engine as he waited for the electric gates to
open. Before they were fully open, he let out
the clutch and roared out onto the road,
narrowly missing a cyclist as he swung left
and accelerated away. Mrs Baines spoke into
the telephone and sadly retreated into the
house.

I came out of hiding and walked along the wall towards a beech tree with branches which hung low over the entrance to the property. The gates were almost closed, but I already had the measure of where a car needed to stop to allow them to open. Thanks to Ting Ling, I had a plan.

****

Early morning sunlight filtered through the leaves of the beech tree, but I was well hidden.

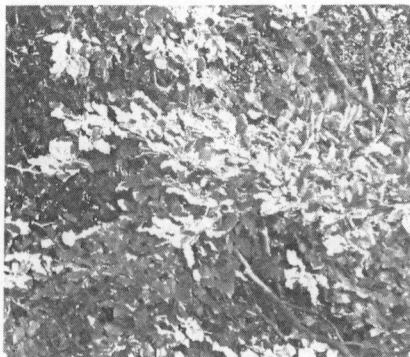

Taking no chances, I had arrived and crept out along my selected branch before sunrise. I saw no other cats on my way through the gardens, but had a feeling Ting Ling was watching as I used her fence to jump up onto the Baines' wall.

After 6am the occasional car drove past, but this was not a through road and nowhere near as busy as the street outside our house. Two people in a silver hatchback drove slowly past at about 7am and returned a few minutes later. I was intrigued when the same car drove slowly past again at about 7. 30 am, but when it stopped outside a house further down the road, I lost interest.

Suddenly, there was action! One of the two up and over garage doors began to open. The 4x4 roared into life from within and emerged into the sunlight. Was Benton in the car? It was impossible to see from my position, so I was relieved when Mr Baines got out. He was wearing a pink shirt and voluminous charcoal trousers held up by broad, bright blue braces. He looked like a clown. No jacket

- no tie - and no respect for Benton! I was getting very angry! The front door of the house opened and a tearful Mrs Baines led Benton out. Give him his due, Benton seemed very calm, although by the way Mrs Baines was trying to stifle a sob, I'm sure he knew what lay in store.

Mr Baines opened the back of the 4x4, strode over to Mrs Baines, snatched the lead from her hand and dragged Benton to the car. I was willing Benton to turn and give him a good biting, but obedient as ever, he jumped dutifully into the back of the car. Mr Baines slammed the door shut and wiped his hands together - job done! As far as he was concerned, Benton's fate was sealed, but not if I could help it!

As he walked to the driver's door he told Mrs Baines to stop sniveling and reminded her that a table had been booked at a fashionable restaurant for a slap-up lunch. The red mist started to descend, but I fought to control it. I had to stay calm if I was to carry out my plan! Mr Baines had to suffer!

He almost took me by surprise. The engine had been left running and as he heaved himself into the driving seat he pressed the accelerator. The big car lurched forward, but of course it had to stop to allow the gates to open, and with a screech of brakes, it stopped precisely where I had predicted.

Now it was a question of timing. I carefully watched the gates as they began to swing open. I only had the one opportunity - get it wrong and it would be good bye Benton!

The gates opened in unison, but I concentrated solely on the right hand one as it inched ever closer to the pattern in the brick paving I had selected as my marker. As it reached the appointed brick, I dropped onto the roof of the 4x4, landing with a satisfying thump at the very moment when Mr Baines stamped his foot on the accelerator.

Pivoting through 180 degrees, I slid backwards down the windscreen directly in front of him, scratching and spitting!

I heard the roar of the engine and saw the look of horror on his face as he involuntarily jerked back to get away from me, an action which caused him to press even harder on the accelerator. The big car careered out through the gateway and was still gaining speed as it smashed into a lamp-post on the other side of the street!

There is a belief that cats always land on their feet. I'm not sure that always holds true, but I'm thankful it worked on that day.

I jumped off the doomed car and was in mid-air a split second before impact. Propelled by the car's momentum I landed on the pavement – running! Fortunately, a garden gate had been left open and weaving through it, I was halfway up the garden path before I had any real control. I crept back and peered out from under the garden hedge to look at the result of my handiwork.

The 4x4 had hit the lamp-post square on. The front of the car was stove in,and the bonnet had sprung open. The lamp-post, leaning at a drunken angle, looked as if it was growing out of the engine compartment, which was enveloped in steam. In the car, Mr Baines was slumped over the steering wheel. I felt rather pleased with myself!

The couple from the silver hatchback were running up the street. The man stopped to take photographs with an expensive looking camera. The young woman continued, talking into a cell phone as she ran. She arrived at the rear of the vehicle at the same time as Mrs Baines and I heard her say she had called for an ambulance. She seemed to know Mrs Baines and they both appeared more concerned about Benton than Mr Baines.

The young woman, who turned out to be Moira, the junior reporter from 'The Echo', opened the back of the 4x4 and Benton jumped out, wagging his tail. The man with the camera was on hand to capture the moment before checking on Mr Baines.

"I think he's alright - I can feel a pulse."

Mrs Baines looked in through the door. "Serves himself right," she said bitterly. "Can't tell him anything. Always in too much of a hurry to fasten his seat belt."

Moira peered in. "At least the airbag went off, but I don't think we should attempt to move him, best wait until the ambulance arrives."

Trailing his lead, Benton took the opportunity to walk over to where I was hiding. "Thanks, Little Buddy," he whispered.

"You're welcome," I whispered back. "Vince said one good turn deserves another - even if ya are a dawg!"

Benton chuckled at my impression. "How is he?"

"He's going to be fine, but not fit enough for this mission. What about you? Will you run away?"

Benton shook his head. "Not an option for a dog, they catch us and we're returned to our owners."

"What are you doing over there Benton?" Benton looked towards Mrs Baines."

"She's alright," he said out of the side of his mouth. "She wants to give me to Moira. Sorry about this, Little Buddy."

Benton cocked his leg, before sauntering back to join the group around the car.

"Did he get you?"

Ting Ling took me by surprise. How had she managed to creep up so quietly?

"No, he missed me on purpose."

"How could dog miss you on purpose, when dogs have no purpose?"

The sirens of approaching emergency vehicles, interrupted my pithy reply.

As the paramedics assessed the condition of Mr Baines, the police closed the road and began to ask questions.

We heard Mrs Baines tell a policewoman that her husband always revved the engine of his car, but this time it kept on revving and he shot across the street into the lamp-post.

A paramedic told the policewoman that the driver had regained consciousness, but he had a broken leg and they had to take great care in moving him in case he had suffered a spinal injury.

The policewoman lent into the car and spoke to Mr Baines. "Do you have any recollection of how the accident happened, sir?"

Mr Baines grimaced in pain. "It was a cat."

"You tried to avoid a cat?"

Mr Baines looked at her as if she was an imbecile. "Of course not! I would never swerve to miss a cat! The cat attacked the car!"

The policewoman smiled. "Big one was it, sir? Lion? Tiger? Leopard? Perhaps a Panther? There have been reports of Panther sightings, but not in this neighborhood."

"No, nothing like that. It was a tabby."

The policewoman opened her notebook and wrote - 'A tabby cat attacked 4x4 and caused accident.' She closed the notebook.

"Been drinking have we sir?"

Mr Baines groaned and closed his eyes.

Eventually the paramedics had Mr Baines strapped to a stretcher and carried him to the ambulance.

Ting Ling whispered. "Man with no patience - now patient."

CHAPTER EIGHT: A MOVING EXPERIENCE

Mr and Mrs Jenks had barely turned their car out onto the road before I poked my head through the cat flap and called out.

"Hi Vince, it's me. Permission to come in?"

"Sure thing, Little Buddy. I'm upstairs - front room - on the computer."

I found Vince sitting on the computer keyboard. The computer was switched off and he was using the monitor as a mirror to examine his 'lampshade contraption'.

"I've worked it out, little Buddy. With ya help I should be able t' git outta this darn thing,"

I jumped up next to him. He turned his head so I could examine the fastening. "See where that tab is tucked into the loop? If ya can use ya computer claw to ease that out, then take it in your teeth and pull it sideways, we should be in business."

I did as instructed. There was a loud ripping sound - I stopped pulling.

"Don't stop Little Buddy! It's meant to make that noise, that's how we know it's coming apart. My folks have been taking it off so as I can eat - then fixing it back on again. Easy for them, but not for me - not being able to see an all. C'mon - give it a good tug. "

I gave a long heave - ignored the loud ripping - and suddenly, the contraption sprang open and fell away. Vince swiped it to the floor with a contemptuous paw and stretched his neck.

"Phew! Thanks for that. When ma folks see I ain't chewed on ma own leg, perhaps they'll leave it off."

I looked at the leg. The bandage had been removed to reveal a mass of stitches crossing over each other and running off in different directions.

"Yup, looks a mess, but it feels good. I'll give it a good licking later - try to get what fur's left going in the right direction to cover the stitches. One has one's pride, don't ya know?"

He smiled at his impression of an Englishman, ambled across the room and, with some difficulty, scrambled up onto the window sill.

"Getting there Little Buddy," he muttered, hiding the pain.

The window sill was partly in shadow. He chose the sunny end, stretching out his injured leg to gain full benefit from the sun's warming rays. "Ah, that's better. Now what's happening with Benton?"

I jumped up and told him how I caused Mr Baines to have an accident. That Benton had a temporary reprieve. How Ting Ling's riddles drove me mad, but her prediction came true.

Vince chuckled. "Yup, she sure drives ya crazy but as ya say, she called it right. Did I ever tell ya how she came by her name?"

I shrugged. "An old Siamese name?"

Vince chuckled some more. "Wrong, Little Buddy - wrong! You flatter her folks - yet you don't flatter her folks."

His gravelly imitation of Ting Ling was hopeless and he knew it. He grinned. "Her folks called her Tiger Lily, but a kitten less like a tiger you never did see! Although she did terrorize the bird population. So, because her folks encourage birds into their garden, they put a collar with a bell around her neck. Never helped the birds, but we could hear her, and that's when we started calling her, Ting Ling. Course, her folks don't know that, they still call her Tiger Lily."

"Like mine still call me Lettuce."

"Well, I can understand how your folks don't realize that you're known in the cat fraternity as Little Buddy, but you would've thought Ting Ling's folks might have cottoned on. But, getting back to Benton. You've done well and I'm mighty proud of ya, but is he still in danger?"

"I overheard Mrs Baines tell Mr Baines that the junior reporter from the Echo wanted to buy him. But Mr Baines is set on having him put down, that's why I did all I could to stop him getting to the vet. It would have been nice if the crash had killed him."

"You, Little Buddy, are one hell of a blood thirsty tabby!" He grinned. "Don't get me wrong, he deserves the pain, but maybe - just maybe - death would've been too easy for him."

I thought on what he said. "You mean it would deprive us of the opportunity to inflict more pain?"

"Precisely, Little Buddy, but first of all we have to make sure Benton is safe."

"Ting Ling has promised to keep an eye on things. Problem is, Benton seems resigned to whatever Mr Baines has in store for him."

"That's the trouble with dawgs - misguided loyalty." Vince paused, his leg was moving into shadow as the sun moved around the house. He dragged himself along the window sill to take advantage of the last patch of sunlight, looked down the street - then looked again! "How long has that been there?"

I followed his gaze to the estate agent's FOR SALE board which had appeared in our front garden while I was saving Benton. I looked at it and my mouth dropped open. The serious implication which went with that sign had not registered.

"Watch and learn, Little Buddy. Your folks are on the move - and that means you! But, there could be months before you go, they've gotta find a buyer first. Have a root around on your folks computer, there's likely to be something about the house sale on there, but, whenever it happens, we're gonna have to have plans in place to keep in touch"

Vince was right about finding the house information on the computer, Jessica had opened a 'House Sale' file, but he was wrong about having to sell before we could move. There would be no need. - Jessica had inherited a house in the country!

When I reported back, Vince set out a plan of action. Saving Benton was a priority, but so was the need to establish a way to secretly communicate by email, or maybe, even Skype? The following day, after Jessica and Toby left for work, Vince came in and set about the task. Jessica had left our computer switched on, although that would never be a problem as Vince had shown me how to switch it on and off. He entered the encrypted part of the computer set up for me and searched to find the location of our new home. An arrow showed where it was on a map and the route to take from our home in Bloomfield Road. It was 36 miles away, probably less, he said, for a cat not restricted to roads. I thought it would be a long hike to get back to my old stamping ground, but Vince reckoned that if a human can walk at 4 miles per hour, an average of 6 miles per hour would be nothing for a cat. He would definitely pay me a visit.

Following several attempts, he registered a unique identity and opened an email account for me in that name. Then he sent himself an email and ran next door to check it had arrived in his secret in-box. He returned within a couple of minutes to show me how to open his reply and respond to it. His leg was definitely getting better!

I discovered that our moving date was to be only three weeks from the day the estate agent's sign appeared in our front garden. In what little time we had left, Vince and I had to ensure Benton's safety and work out a suitable punishment for Mr Baines.

On the Thursday of that week. I paid my daily visit to Ting Ling. She was sitting on her fence and told me, in her usual sing-song way, that there was nothing to report. Benton was still at home and Mr Baines was still in hospital. As I turned to leave, she called after me.

"Thursday - you see later - broken car is in the paper!"

"Yeah - thanks Ting Ling. See you tomorrow!"

That weird cat was driving me crazy. Probably a good job I was moving; it wouldn't do to kill one of your own species!

Vince was stretched out on his patio, enjoying the warmth of the late summer sun as I jumped up onto the back fence. A slight movement of a massive paw indicated that he had seen me and it was alright to enter his domain. A few cats had tried to take liberties, only to discover that a convalescing Vince was still more than a match for them."Any news?""Benton's still there. And Mr Baines is still in hospital. Ting Ling said something about a car in a paper - one of her stupid riddles." Vince rolled onto his feet and walked stiffly towards his cat flap. "Can ya remember the riddle?"I thought hard. "It was something like...Thursday seeing later...then...broken car is in the paper." He turned his head and grinned. You underestimate her, Little Buddy - take a look at this."I followed him through his cat flap and onto the kitchen table. The weekly edition of 'The Echo', published every Thursday, was on the table. A photograph of the wrecked Baines 4x4 on the front page under the headline, "DRIVER BLAMES BIG CAT!" And in bold print under the picture - Full story on page 7. Vince used his computer claw to flick through to where the whole page was devoted to an Exclusive Report by Moira Jones, 'Staff Reporter'. Which was good news for Moira, she had been a 'Junior Reporter' the previous week. In her report she told readers that she happened to be in the vicinity, gathering evidence to support her theory that cats could have been responsible for the death of a fox on the Bloomfield estate, when the accident occurred. She heard the roar of an engine and saw a 4x4 drive out at great speed from Bloomfield House, and smash into a lamp post on the other side of the road. She called the emergency services as she and Echo photographer, Clive Butler, ran to offer assistance. They were first on the scene, closely followed by Mrs Sylvia Baines, wife of the driver, Mr Desmond Baines. The driver was alive but unconscious. Due to the severity of the impact, and the fact that Mr Baines had not been wearing a seat-belt, although air bags had deployed, they thought it best to leave him in the car until the emergency services arrived.

Police and paramedics were quickly on the scene. Mr Baines regained consciousness before being transferred to an ambulance and told WPC Emily Strut, that the accident had been caused by a large, cat like creature which attacked his car.

Mr Baines has a broken leg and due to unspecified internal injuries, remains in hospital under observation.

From the tone of the piece, it seemed obvious the reporter was skeptical about the cause of the accident, but having chanced upon an opportunity to advance her career, she was going to milk the story for all it was worth. She concluded her piece by emphasizing that although there had been reported sightings of a black panther during the summer months, those sightings had been in distant rural areas and not substantiated. However, something had been responsible for the death of the fox and a prowling Big Cat could be the culprit. She promised her readers that she would continue with her investigations. Best of luck to her, I thought, at least she was on our side. As I read I became conscious of Vince watching me. I looked up. He was grinning.

"How d'ya manage t' turn ya self into a BIG CAT, Little Buddy?

CHAPTER NINE: MISSION ACCOMPLISHED

The following day, Vince decided to test his leg by accompanying me to Bloomfield House.

Ting Ling appeared on the fence at the bottom of Vince's garden as we were about to leave and although Vince walked quickly down the garden to meet her, it was possible to detect a slight limp.

Ting Ling gave him a nervous, cross eyed smile. "Good to see you walking well - cat with no limp..."

Vince held a large paw aloft to stop her. "No riddles, Ting Ling. What's wrong?"

Ting Ling moved uneasily on the fence. "Bad news - Benton gone."

"Gone where?"

Ting Ling shrugged. "I hear door slam and car drive away. Jumping up on wall I see Mrs Baines with handkerchief - drying tears. I jump down and rub against her legs. I like Mrs Baines - yet not like Mr Baines."

"Git on with it!" growled Vince.

"She looked down at me and sobbed, 'He's gone, Tiger Lily.' She calls me Tiger Lily because that is the name my ..."

"We know that Ting Ling!" I snapped, "just tell us what she said."

"I am telling," said Ting Ling defiantly. "Mrs Baines said he had gone, then ran crying into house."

"Did she say it was Benton that had gone?" asked Vince.

"Could it be that Mr Baines has died?" I asked eagerly.

Ting Ling turned her attention to me and shook her head. "You one blood thirsty tabby - you know that?"

"Yes," I said, "Vince has told me many times."

Ting Ling sniffed. "Sorry to disappoint, but definitely Benton, Mrs Baines not cry over Mr Baines."

Vince pondered on the news."Thanks, Ting Ling, but if ya don't mind, Little Buddy and I will wander over to see if we can pick up some clues."

"No problem, Vince. Sure you make it?"

Ting Ling was looking doubtfully at Vince's leg, which to any cat who hadn't seen it when he first came home looked, as Vince himself admitted, one hell of a mess!

"Thanks for your concern, Ting Ling, I'll get there, but at a walk rather than a run. You go first, we'll follow."

Vince struggled a little with jumping, but the strength in his front legs saw him over every obstacle and the step to the Bloomfield House wall from the shed in the neighboring garden was achieved with ease. We walked along the wall in full view of the house.

Surely, if Benton was at home, there would be some sort of reaction? Vince looked at me. "D'ya remember Benton's scent, Little Buddy?"

I nodded. "Yup - I think so, though it's not as strong as Reynard's."

"In Reynard's case ya smelt his blood - which ain't surprising since you was covered in it!. With Benton ya would have detected his pheromones. Much subtler, but distinctive to Benton. I need ya to go down into the garden and check; find recent pheromones and we'll know he's still around."

"Or not around," added Ting Ling.

"Git!" growled Vince.

Not sure if he was speaking to me, or Ting Ling, I jumped down into the garden.

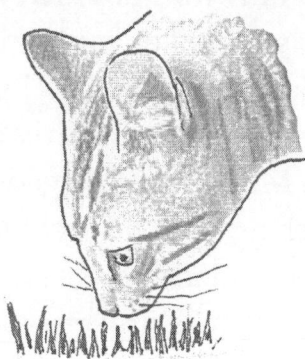

After spending over half an hour sniffing around in the garden, I was unable to reach a conclusion.

Vince sent Ting Ling to the front of the house as a lookout and jumped gingerly down into the garden to join me. I took him to the spots where I could smell traces of Benton, and Vince confirmed what I was thinking; there was nothing recent - Benton had gone!

Reluctantly, we climbed up through the evergreen shrub to the top of the wall and sat morosely looking over what had been Benton's domain. I desperately wanted to make Mr Baines suffer – but time was running out – fast!

With only four days left to our move, Ting Ling appeared on our garden fence with the news that Mr Baines was home! An ambulance drove into the drive of Bloomfield House and Mr Baines emerged from the back in a wheelchair, with his right leg in plaster.

The ambulance driver watched in horror as Mr Baines drove at full speed

towards the front door which Mrs Baines opened, just in time.

He narrowly missed her as the wheel chair bumped over the threshold. All this happened only a few minutes before. I had to get over there, and fast!

Vince counseled caution.

"Take it easy, Little Buddy. You've got a few days yet. Mr Baines will have to develop new routines. Take time to watch and learn. Watch, learn and be careful, he may have a replacement for Benton, a new dawg could arrive at any time."

I knew Vince was right, and he couldn't be there to help if I got myself in a fix. During our trip to check on Benton he pulled some stitches - his leg needed more time to heal.

I promised not to do anything hasty and set off for Bloomfield House with Ting Ling, who gave me her advice.

"Mr Baines deserve all he get - yet perhaps he is not deserving."

I ignored her - Ting Ling was making me cross!

I sat on the wall behind the feathery tops of the golden junipers watching and listening, and soon realized I could hear the whine of the electric motor on his wheelchair, even when he was in the house.

Later, on that first day, he came out onto the patio where I could see how he operated the wheelchair with a small stick by his right hand. A ramp had been placed on one side of the steps leading down to the lawn and when Mrs Baines came out onto the patio at about 2pm, Mr Baines drove the wheelchair down the ramp and Mrs Baines followed him down the garden to the fish pond, where he fed his fish.

On the second day, I recognized the wheelchair sounds before it appeared on the patio. Once again it was about 2 pm, only this time Mr Baines drove the wheelchair down the garden to feed the fish on his own.

I watched his progress carefully, and worked out my plan of action. Tomorrow would be the day!

I took my place on the wall behind the golden junipers before noon, and waited patiently. If everything went to plan, this day would see Mr Baines pay the ultimate price for his callous treatment of Benton.

But, 'the best laid plans of mice and men' –
that's a quote I picked up from Vince – why
mice? Why not cats or even dogs? Anyway, at
1pm it began to rain and by 2pm, what started
as drizzle had turned into a downpour. I
heard stomping movements from within the
house, not the wheelchair's electric motor. By
4pm it became obvious that Mr Baines was not
going to feed his fish. Wet, bedraggled, and
frustrated, I slouched off home.

I don't know what made me adopt
Vince's silent entry method to go through my
own cat flap. Perhaps it was something to do
with that sixth sense Vince had once told me
about? Whatever, I entered a house littered
with packed boxes. Jessica and Toby had been
very busy. They were still at it, I could hear
them in the lounge. I heard my name
mentioned and crept closer. They were
arguing, and as usual, Toby was on my case.

"I think we should put her into her cage
as soon as she comes in. We'll never catch her
tomorrow - you know what she's like."

"She'll be alright, Toby. Lettuce always
comes when I call."

"But if she doesn't?"

"She will - she always does."

"Yes, but not when she knows we are moving."

"How could she possibly know?"

"Look at the place, Jess. She must suspect something. If you want to risk leaving your beloved Lettuce behind, it's entirely up to you."

Jessica gave a big sigh. "Oh, alright then, but on your head be it. If she gives you a scratch, don't come complaining to me."

Having heard enough, I crept back into the kitchen, past my food bowl, which had been filled with fishy bites, one of my favorites. I was tempted, but it was impossible to eat them without loud crunching.

I left as silently as I arrived and jumped over the fence at the back of garage into the neighboring garden. It was no good sneaking in to see Vince - that was the first place Toby would look. Time to make myself scarce!

The Baines wall, where it ran under the eaves of their garage provided a dry place to spend the night.

Throughout the remaining hours of daylight and well into the evening, I heard both Toby and Jessica calling me, but with paws over my ears, I snuggled down for a fitful sleep.

I awoke to the dawn chorus with pangs of hunger but no interest in birds, only my mission: to make Mr Desmond Baines suffer for his treatment of Benton!

The rain had stopped so I decided to take up my position behind the junipers and lay low. I expected to wait for at least 8 hours, which is nothing for a cat. But, at 10am, when I was lazily stretched out on my back enjoying the morning sun, I heard the unmistakable sound of the wheelchair moving around inside the house. Eyes closed, I tried to picture where Mr Baines could be, but when I heard the short sharp whines from the electric motor which I associated with tight man oeuvres around furniture, I was on my feet and alert. The motor changed to a constant whine - he was moving down their long room towards the patio doors!

I peered through juniper fronds to see Mrs Baines opening the doors. There was no break in the whine of the electric motor and she had to move smartly to one side as the wheel chair bounced over the threshold and headed across the patio for the ramp to the garden.

Mr Baines was wearing a short sleeved shirt and a straw hat, so it looked as if he intended to spend some time in the sun. I recognized the box on his lap as the one which contained fish food. I was in luck!

As the wheel chair sped past, I jumped down from the wall, and followed. Although he was driving at full speed, it was easy for me to keep up. I had considered waiting until he stopped by the pond, but decided an attack on the move would provide a better chance of success.

As he skirted the circular rose bed, I began my run. When Mr Baines was twelve yards from the pond I was airborne. Ten yards and I landed on his shoulder. Eight and I was in his face, spitting and yowling. Five and he was screaming and pulling back on the control stick. Four and I was on his forearm, my computer claw dug into the back of his hand pushing it forward. Two yards and I spun through 180 degrees to leap back onto his shoulder. I saw the fear in his eyes before he turned his head away to shield his face. But, one yard and I was airborne again, leaving Mr Baines desperately trying to regain control of the wheelchair, but too late!

The small wheels at the front dipped into the water and although the electric motor was now in reverse, the rear wheels found no traction. Mr Baines and the wheelchair slid down into the inky depths to join his beloved fish. I scrambled up through the evergreen shrub onto the wall, and looked down on the pond

Mr Baines straw hat was floating serenely on the surface. Then I heard shouting. Mrs Baines was running down the garden. Time to leave the scene of the crime!

Keeping low I worked my way through the gardens, but when I heard Jessica calling, I altered my route and emerged in the front garden of number 57 Bloomfield Road.

Cautiously peering around a gate post, I saw a large removals van parked in the road outside my house. The back doors were open, men busy loading. Keeping under cover, I crept closer. I wanted to give Vince the good news before I was caught and caged!

I paused in the hedge between numbers 47 and 45, the next piece of cover would be the hedge where Vince implicated me in the attack on our postman. The action which saw me gain an undeserved reputation, seemed a long time ago. I chuckled to myself at the memory. Who would have thought that a callow kitten would go on to become a serial killer?

"What's so amusing, Little Buddy?" Vince was hiding in the shadows beneath his family car. "Wanna come under here - they're looking for ya."

I moved along the hedge until the car was between me and the loading activity at the back of the removals van, and slipped under the car to join him.

"I heard them calling, but I've got something important to tell you, before they whisk me off in that cage."

Vince nodded grimly. "Yup. The time is nigh, Little Buddy, but I've got some good news to send ya on your way - Benton is alive."

"Huh?" My jaw dropped, but Vince continued.

"Yup. We had a visit from Moira, the reporter from the local newspaper. She wanted to find out about my leg and when I got the injury. My folks told her all she wanted to know, and as I found it all a mite embarrassing, I wandered around to the front of the house and there he was – Benton, sitting in the back of Moira's hatchback, rear door wide open, on guard!

Benton grinned at my surprise and I told him we thought he had been put down. He said that was what he was expecting, even after the accident you engineered. Then something completely unexpected happened. Mr Baines phoned from the hospital and told Mrs Baines to sell Benton to Moira for one penny. Mr Baines had what they call an epiphany, Little Buddy. So he's not such a bad guy after all. Hope you didn't rough him up too much?"

Oops! From the high of the kill, I suddenly felt deflated - it couldn't be true.

"Are you sure? I mean - has he really changed?"

"Yup, even told Mrs Baines she could have a cat. Now that's what I call, a real epiphany."

"Lettuce! Lettuce darling!" Jessica was calling from the back garden.

"Lettuce! Lettuce! Where are you, you little perisher?" Toby was calling from the front.

Time was fast running out. I looked guiltily at Vince. "Vince - I feel dreadful, I ....."

Vince shrugged. "Don't worry about it, Little Buddy. If they wanted an obedient pet, they should have bought a dawg.

Now git!"

CHAPTER TEN: WALNUT TREE FARM

As the removals van left, Toby dumped the cage, with me inside, unceremoniously onto the back seat of the car. Jessica said I was a very naughty cat. If only she knew! Toby was mad and would not speak directly to me. Jessica put a seat belt around the cage. Toby said if it crashed to the floor and I was hurt, it would serve me right. Neither had offered me any food, or water. I would send an email on the subject to the RSPCA, that would teach them a lesson!

If you are a human, and would like to know how much a cat can see from the back of a car, try putting your head down on the seat instead of your bottom. I can tell you - you won't get much of a view!

I decided that rather than listen to Toby's stupid prattle, I would have a doze. Dunking Mr Baines in the fish pond - although technically speaking, I suppose if you dunk someone, you take them back out again: anyway - dunking or drowning, whatever you prefer to call it, is a very tiring business.

"Here we are, Lettuce. Walnut Tree Farm!" I woke with a start. I had seen a picture of the house so knew what to expect - but it was the fifteen acres which intrigued me. Vince reckoned that it would be one hell of a lot of roaming space. But it soon became evident that Toby wanted me left in my cage until, as he put it, I could identify with my new surroundings. Have these people never heard of Google Earth?

While Toby walked out onto the lane to wait for the removals van, Jessica carried the cage to the back of the house and set me down on a table under a walnut tree.

It was a large tree, great to climb and hide in, but it didn't lead anywhere. There was no wall to drop down onto - and more importantly, no neighboring garden. I was missing Vince already, and vowed that as soon as I was free, I would high tail it back to Bloomfield Road.

Jessica came back with a bowl of water and a dish of fishy bites, which she pushed into the cage through a narrow horizontal door. They were taking no chances!

My imprisonment was to last for five days. Not in the cage it is true, but imprisonment nonetheless.

When the removals van left, I was taken inside and set down on bare floorboards in a small upstairs room. Jessica told me it was for my own good. Then she brought up my bed, my litter tray, which I had not used since I was a kitten, and some of my old toys. As if I would be interested in pouncing on Dipper, after my killing spree?

She opened the cage and made a hasty retreat, closing the door to the room firmly behind her.

It was boring in that room. I could hear lots of banging and scraping as furniture was brought in and moved about. I spent most of my time, looking out through the window which was at the back of the house. Not a lot to see, only fields and large black birds with enormous beaks, the like of which I had never seen in our garden at Bloomfield Road. At night, strange animals moved through the field. I caught a glimpse of a fox but not a single cat; which I thought rather strange. On the fourth day I heard a vehicle, which sounded like the removals van, drive into the yard by the side of the house. I pressed my nose hard against the window, expecting it to come into view but it stopped and I heard a heavy metallic crash. Jessica ran out from the back door, wearing some very strange trousers and long boots. Then I heard a terrible clattering noise and would not have been surprised to see her run back indoors again. But no, she seemed pleased and excited as she disappeared around the side of the house. I heard more frantic clattering which settled down to a rhythmic clash, as Jessica re-appeared leading an enormous black creature, which she took into a field.

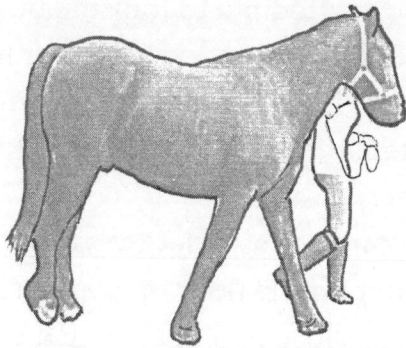

The creature showed enormous teeth as Jessica pressed her face against the side of its head. I was sure it was going to eat her, but she patted its neck and for some strange reason, it let her walk away. Then it tossed its enormous head, made an incredibly shrill sound for such a large creature, and ran off down the field at great speed.

Ha, I thought, the lucky devil is going to get away! But no, it ran around the field several times and came back to the gate where Jessica was waiting with an apple, which it ate! What sort of creature would want to eat an apple?

That evening, Jessica opened the door to my jail and invited me to tour the house. Apparently I had been locked in for my own good, but having arranged the furniture as they wanted, they now had time to keep an eye on me.

She carried my litter tray downstairs and placed it on the floor of a large room with a stone floor, close to a door which was fitted with a cat flap. Yippee! Freedom! I charged at it full tilt. It was locked! Dazed, I turned to see Toby laughing at me. Jessica was more understanding

"I'll take you out and show you around tomorrow, Lettuce. It's a big wide open space out there, we don't want you getting lost."

"Speak for yourself," said Toby. "That cat's trouble. I've been saying so for ages."

"No she's not, are you darling?" I shut my eyes, as if in ecstasy - enjoying the fuss. In fact I was plotting pay back time for Toby.

"There we are, let me show you around your new home." Cradling me in her arms, Jessica walked me through the ground floor. I recognized some of the old furniture, but it was spread thinly in such a large house. Jessica seemed to pick up on my thoughts.

"We're going to have some new furniture, we'll soon have the place comfortable and cozy." I squirmed in her arms. She thought I understood, but in fact I was anxious to see where they had set up the computer. The last room downstairs, or so I thought was a large room, which she called their lounge. Hmm, very nice, but where had they stashed the computer?

We were back to the stairs, but she went past them and into what in our old house would have been the under-stairs cupboard, but this door led into another room. A long room with a floor to ceiling bookcase along a wall opposite three large windows with deep low sills.

"This is the oldest part of the house," she said proudly. "Those are sash windows, they're Georgian and they let in lots of light, that's why this is the library. We're going to fill all those shelves with books."

"Yippee!" Not the books, the computer! It was set up against the wall to the left of the windows.

I thought the deep window sills, which looked out over the driveway into Walnut Tree Farm, would make a comfy spot to watch people come and go. I would also get good warning of arrivals, when using the computer.

There was another door, in the corner where the computer wall met the bookcase. It was slightly open and I hoped this would always be the case, otherwise I might have difficulty gaining access. Jessica carried me out through that door and we were back in the large hall by the front entrance, and the stairs.

She put me down and I followed her into the kitchen. To the right there was a small hall and door which opened into a walk-in larder. I know because I walked in after her. She took some food pouches for me from a shelf, emptied them into a dish and put it down in a small hallway between the larder and another outside door - and another cat flap. I tested it with a paw. It was locked.

Jessica smiled down at me. "Tomorrow darling. I'll take you outside tomorrow, but for now you can go anywhere in the house."

I had a good sniff around the small hall way. Another cat had been there; but a long time ago. I ate my food and had a slurp of water. Jessica watched from the kitchen where she had been joined by Toby. I went and brushed against her legs, completely ignoring him, and to demonstrate my independence, wandered off through the dining room, into the front hall and up the stairs. I found their bed in a large room, used my claws to check if it was still soft and comfy and curled up in the middle for a digestive nap.

Jessica kept her promise and took me outside on the fifth day, but not until she had already been out, wearing those weird trousers and high boots. It was late morning before she came back for me. She smelt very strange, a strong smell, almost as bad as Reynard! She carried me into the yard with the wooden sheds.

The head of the large black creature was poking out over a low door in one of them. As we approached it made the same shrill noise I heard the previous day.

"This is Jake, my horse." Jessica held me close to the long black nose. Jake snorted hot air over me through cavernous nostrils.

"He likes you, Lettuce darling."

I thought not, there was something wild about those eyes, and he reeked of that strong odor I was beginning to associate with Jessica's weird trousers. Then, she confirmed a growing suspicion.

"Toby bought him for me. I've always wanted my own horse, and now we have our own stables and meadows, I can. You'll see me groom him, much as I groom you, but it will take a lot longer. Then we'll go for long rides in the countryside."

I quite liked it when Jessica brushed my fur, but with Jake to groom, and looking at the size of him, I could immediately see she would have little time for me. It was all part of Toby's plan to alienate me from Jessica. The horse would have to go! I unleashed my computer claw and dabbed him on the nose, only to make him aware of my intentions, but he went ballistic!

That put paid to my guided tour of the estate, not that I minded. I was desperate to get on the computer and make contact with Vince. The problem was, both Jessica and Toby had taken time off work for the move and as far as I could gather, they had another week to go. Getting on the computer while they were around was too risky. I was still in Jessica's bad books, which seemed to suit Toby, who took great delight in reminding me that both cat flaps were locked, as they left to go shopping.

He had no idea as I watched them drive off and he gave me a sarcastic wave, that the library was exactly where I wanted to be!

I waited until I heard the car turn out onto the main road, and accelerate away, before jumping down from the window sill and up next to the computer. It was switched on. Toby had been using it while Jessica cleaned out the stable and groomed Jake.

I followed the procedure Vince taught me and logged into my secret user file. I had several emails - all from Vince. The first was short - simply to make contact and say he would be checking his emails. The second was longer and dated the day following our move.

Hi Little Buddy - Overheard my folks talking about Mr Baines this morning. Seems he drowned in his own fish pond. He drove his wheel chair down there to feed his beloved fish. Police seem to think it was an accident. Seems strange to me, what with you determined to teach him a lesson 'n all. Thinking back, was ya trying to tell me something before Toby came along? Happy hunting - Vince

The third message was dated two days after our move.

Hi Little Buddy - Ting Ling has just paid me a visit. Seems she saw it all, said it was really impressive. Your attack timed to perfection. Don't worry. How could you have known about his change of heart? The whole cat community on the Bloomfield Estate are 100% behind ya. Your secret is safe with us. And remember, Benton would only be a memory without your intervention.

Happy hunting - Vince

The fourth message arrived yesterday.

> Worried about lack of contact. If I don't hear from ya soon, we may have to send someone to check you out. Sandy from number 15 is on standby. Can't risk 36 miles with my leg as it is. We'll give you another 3 days. Hope all is OK - Vince.

I flicked out my computer claw and tapped on 'reply'.

Hi Vince - Sorry I've not been in touch. Unable to get on computer until now. If there are future communication delays it will be because Toby and Jessica are around. They've taken time off work for the move. Sorry I could not tell you about Mr Baines before Toby arrived. Everything OK now, although Toby is determined to make me pay for evading capture prior to our departure. Have been locked in the house, but have identified an escape route. Jessica has a horse which could be a problem. His name is Jake - any idea how I could get rid of a horse? Please thank Sandy for standing by, but no longer required. Happy hunting- Little Buddy

I sent the message on its way. Checked to make sure it had gone, closed my files and had a little nosy to see what Toby had been up to.

A site for agricultural machinery had been visited, and another for a Tractor Auction which was due to take place in a couple of days time. If Jessica went with him, or went riding on Jake, it would present an ideal opportunity to get back on the computer.

I left everything as I found it and went upstairs to what Jessica referred to as the family bathroom, although I was the only family and it was hardly my scene. The door to the bathroom was half open, and it led to freedom! Investigation had revealed a small window propped open, which looked out over fields, and most importantly a sloping roof.

It was an easy means of escape so I took myself on the tour of Walnut Tree Farm, as promised by Jessica.

The farm was really no more than four large fields, although some had been divided up into smaller enclosures, which I would learn were called paddocks, a term used by people with horses.

Jake was in one of the paddocks - eating grass. Grass? He looked up as I sauntered past. Lifting his head high he made that shrill noise of his and thundered towards me, stopping just short of the fence, nostrils flared, eyes bulging. I jumped back several feet.

I had been thinking that this horse could be more use to me alive than dead. Taking Jessica off on a long ride would help guarantee time on the computer. There was also the thorny problem of how a tabby cat could possibly kill a horse. It was in my interest to cultivate a friendship with Jake.

"Look, I'm sorry Jake. I didn't mean to have a claw out. It was meant as a pat - a way of saying - pleased to meet you."

Jake glowered at me. "Think I was born yesterday? I lived on a farm where we had dogs and they warned me about cats. Get within kicking distance and you're dead."

I stared back at him. "If that's how you want it, that's okay with me, but don't say I didn't extended a paw of friendship."

He moved his head up and down and snorted, sure of his physical superiority. He had no idea what he was dealing with.

I had almost completed my stroll around the perimeter of the farm when I heard their car, the engine protesting as the driver changed down through the gears, before turning into the lane. It had to be Toby! I sprinted from behind the stables, and managed to get out of sight around the corner of the house, as the car screeched into the drive. Jessica called for me when she came in through the front door, and tail up, I walked calmly down the stairs to greet her.

CHAPTER ELEVEN: JUMP JET CAT

Vince told me about the wildlife I could expect to see when we moved to the country. High among them, rabbits, and I could see why. I saw many of them in my stroll around the farm, especially at the bottom of a large field, which sloped down, out of view from the house. It was a place which suited me well, as Toby was still insisting I should be locked in the house.

A rabbit was munching away on something as I stealthily approached. Not another grass eater? I almost felt guilty; it didn't stand a chance, but as I tensed to pounce it was off! I gave chase but that rabbit ran like the wind, ducked into a hole by the hedge and disappeared.

No problem; there were others. I focused my attention on my second rabbit - but the same thing happened - and with the third - and the fourth - and the fifth!

I sat down next to one of the holes. I could smell them, but I couldn't reach them. Time to watch, learn and work out a strategy!

That evening I feigned sleep on Jessica's lap as they discussed plans for the following day. Toby wanted Jessica to accompany him to a farm machinery auction. Jessica wanted to take Jake out for a long ride. Jessica won the argument, which prompted me to pretend to wake up and lick her hand.

"There you are," she said, "even Lettuce thinks my time will be better spent riding Jake, than looking at rusty old tractors."

Toby glowered at me and I smirked. I liked the idea that somehow I had been instrumental in spoiling his day.

The following morning I made myself comfy on my window sill in the library. It was early. I watched Jessica lead Jake in from the field and take him to the stables. He looked mighty pleased with himself, but for now it suited me to let him live, despite the rejection of my friendship. Mind you, knowing Jessica would lavish a large slice of my grooming time on him, was a bitter pill.

"Sometimes sacrifices need to be made for the common good." I could hear Vince saying it - and of course, he was right.

Toby came into the library. I pretended to be asleep as I watched him log onto the computer. He checked his emails before printing out a list of farm machinery for sale at the auction. It covered eight sheets of paper, which he stapled together. Then he went though the lists, using a marker pen to highlight items he was interested in. Satisfied, he rolled up the papers and gave me a sharp tap on the head with them as he marched past. I ignored him.

I heard the car start, and watched as he drove past the entrance to the stables, waving and hooting the car horn. I heard a lot of clattering and clashing and Jake appeared at the entrance with Jessica sitting on his back.

He was jumping up and down and Jessica was holding on for dear life. She did not look very pleased and as I found out later, it was Toby she was not pleased with.

Apparently the one thing you don't do around horses is sound a car horn. Hmm – interesting.

Jessica managed to settle Jake down, and seeing me, gave a cheery wave as she rode him, at a steady walk, down the drive.

They turned right and I watched Jessica's head and shoulders moving down the lane above the hedge. When she was on Jake, she was a long way off the ground, he really was enormous. Perhaps I should give up on any thoughts of toppling him? Either way, that could wait - time for the computer.

Vince had replied to my email.

> Hi Little Buddy – Sandy is disappointed that you have surfaced; he was looking forward to a stroll in the countryside. I can't think of a way to kill a horse apart from Jacobaea vulgaris, commonly known as ragwort, a yellow flowering plant which is supposed to be poisonous for them. But maybe you should wait to see how life with Jake pans out? There's some news provided by Ting Ling, but as yet unsubstantiated – Mr Baines death has been referred to the Coroner. - Good to hear from ya - Vince

What did that mean? I flicked out my computer claw and sent a reply.

Hi Vince - Thanks for your message. Sorry to disappoint Sandy. Take your point about Jake, I have been thinking that he might be of more use to me alive than dead. What does referring a death to the coroner mean? Mr Baines is dead, isn't he? This place is teeming with rabbits. After many attempts, caught one yesterday. Delicious! Will stay on computer for a while to see if you're around. Jessica and Toby out at the moment. Should be at least another couple of hours. Hope to hear from you soon - Little Buddy.

After sending my message, I wandered through to the back hall to see if any food had been left out for me. There was a dish of tasty morsels, but I can't be bribed. As I scrunched into them, they only served as a reminder to send my complaint to the RSPCA. I went back to the computer; no reply from Vince so composed a mischievous message for the RSPCA.

I was snoozing on the window sill, when I heard the ping. An email had arrived! I jumped over to check, hoping it was from Vince. But it was a holding message from the RSPCA to tell me that my email had been received and would be dealt with as soon as possible.

I resumed my position on the window sill and waited, but there was no response from Vince. When I heard Jessica and Jake coming up the lane, I closed my file and went to meet them.

Jake snorted when they turned into the drive and he saw me. I gave him a wide berth and walked into the stable yard with them, tail held high. Jessica was impressed but perplexed.

"How did you manage to get out, Lettuce? I thought Toby locked you in?"

I replied with a little purp and my smile of innocence. Jessica looked at me doubtfully, was she beginning to believe Toby's propaganda? I kept my distance as she dismounted from Jake, who kept a wary eye on me. Jessica hugged his head and rubbed that long nose.

"It's only Lettuce, Jake. She can't do you any harm."

If only she knew! As she tied Jake to a ring on the stable wall, I sauntered across the yard and jumped up into a gap in the hay bales, stored in the barn, opposite. I settled down to watch - watch and learn.

I heard Toby coming long before Jessica, who was grooming Jake. When the car pulled into the yard. Toby jumped out enthusiastically. I eased back a couple of bales and listened from the shadows.

"I got it Jess!"

"The Ferguson?"

"Yes, the one I was after, and at the lower end of the predicted price. Delivery on a low loader next week."

Jessica stopped grooming, walked over to Toby and gave him a kiss on the cheek. "Well done. What about the trailer?"

"Didn't bother. The Fergie's got a box which fits on the back - quite big - I think we might manage with that - we'll see."

"Anything else of interest?"

Toby grinned. "Well there was actually, it's in the back of the car. Want to take a look?"

Jessica looked doubtful. "What have you done now?"

Toby opened the car tail gate and a shaggy brown and white head poked out.

"Not a dog? I thought you said we would choose one together?"

"I know Jess, but this one needs a home. Come on Charlie, come and say hello."

The scruffiest cross breed you could ever imagine, tumbled out from the car and tail wagging furiously, walked over to Jessica. What a creep! And not only the dog! Toby had really crossed the line this time. I would plan carefully. I would watch and learn. Toby would pay the price for bringing that wretched creature to Walnut Tree Farm.

The following day I had a confrontation with Charlie. Like all dogs, he thought barking and running towards a cat, would make them run. However, he had not reckoned on coming up against a cat advised and trained by Vince.

Charlie barked and ran at me in the stable yard. I behaved as most cats would and turned tail. A triumphant Charlie ran after me - and fell into my trap!

Before we left Bloomfield Road, I was pretending to doze as Toby watched a TV program about the Falklands War and the success of Harrier Jump Jets. Now I was about to employ the same principle. I ran full tilt towards one of the paddocks with Charlie in hot pursuit. The rail fencing in a paddock is built to keep horses in, not cats or dogs out. Charlie expected me to run through the gap under the rails, but at the very last moment, I jumped onto the top rail. Charlie hurtled under the lower rail and claws out, I dropped down onto his back; a maneuver any Harrier pilot would be proud of. Then, remembering vividly how Vince rode Benton, I moved forward onto the lower part of Charlie's neck, dug my back claws in for support and sat up, jockey style, to box him about the ears - front claws fully extended - of course!

Yelping with pain, Charlie charged across the field and down to where the rabbits live. They heard him coming and scampered for cover. Charlie followed towards a bramble filled hedge. I dismounted at the critical moment, leaving poor old Charlie to tangle with the brambles.

"You could have bought a brighter dog, Toby?"

Toby looked glumly on as Jessica bathed Charlie's ears. She pointed to the ragged back edge of one ear

"You would have thought he would have stopped as the thorns ripped through this."

"Perhaps he was chasing rabbits and couldn't stop," said Toby, desperately trying to find an excuse for his daft purchase.

I edged closer. Charlie whimpered, wide eyed with fear. Jessica soothed him.

"They'll be alright, Charlie, you must learn to watch where you're going." She dried his ears, applied some antiseptic cream, and shook her head as she looked at Toby.

"As lovely as he is, can you really see him as a guard dog?"

"He's got a good bark. I thought we could put him on a long chain in the yard when we're at work. I'll make a sort of kennel for him between the bales in the hay barn."

Jessica gave him a hard look. "You're not really suggesting we leave him outside all day?"

"He'll be alright, we can put some food and water down for him - and he'll have Jake and Lettuce for company."

"Jake will be out in a paddock most days until winter sets in, and if recent winters are anything to go by, there won't be many days he'll need to be inside. Once Lettuce has settled in, she'll spend most of her time hunting. I could ask Tracy to take him for a walk, she'll be here to muck out Jake's stable and ride him during the week.

Toby insisted in his belief that Charlie would make a good guard dog, and went ahead with his plan.

Charlie seemed to enjoy being outside and having freedom, even if it was limited by the length of the chain. He barked whenever someone drove in.

Toby was off again, buying heavens knows what, and Jessica was riding Jake, as I approached Charlie for a little chat.

"D'ya get the message, Charlie?"

"What message?" Charlie had squeezed back into the gap Toby had created between the bales. He was trying to put on a brave front, but his front legs gave him away. They were quivering. I moved close and lay down, belly exposed, just as Vince had done to Benton. Would Charlie have enough sense not to make a move?

Smiling at him, I rolled over onto my back, pretending my defenses were down. He was tempted, but changed his mind.

"Very wise, Charlie. The message is simple, if you ever tangle with me, you'll come off second best. So, here's the deal. I will tolerate you as long as you do as I command and that may mean going against instructions from Toby or Jessica - especially Toby."

Charlie was horrified. "I couldn't possibly disobey my master or mistress."

"Your choice Charlie. You don't know me very well, so let me spell it out to you. Obey me – it could mean the difference between LIFE OR DEATH."

A puzzled look washed over Charlie's face, starting in his eyes and ending on his sagging lower lip.

"You've got it Charlie. Your life - or your death."

I nonchalantly rolled over onto my feet, and fixed him with a penetrating gaze as I completed the move. Satisfied that the message had been received, I turned my back on him and slowly walked away.

CHAPTER TWELVE: MY WINTER OF DISCONTENT

Toby was expecting delivery of his tractor and moving hay bales in the barn to clear a space for it to stand under cover.

As Jessica was riding Jake, I took the opportunity to check for any messages. There was just the one - from Vince. No real news, other than an inquest into the death of Mr Baines was definitely going ahead. I sent a quick reply to say that Jessica and Toby would be back to work on Monday and I would have a detailed conversation with him then. I closed down and took my usual position on the window sill.

Charlie had been let off his lead and was sniffing about, gradually moving out of the yard towards the paddocks. Toby called him back and Charlie was about to obey when he saw me.

Toby moved the last couple of bales, and rechecked the size of the bay he had created by pacing across, then from back to front. He nodded to himself in satisfaction before speaking to Charlie, but Charlie wasn't there, he was halfway down the field chasing rabbits. Toby ran after him, shouting the rude words usually reserved for me!

Then it began to snow!

The snow lingered on the fields for a couple of days, but it didn't stop Toby trying out his new toy, there were tractor tracks all over the place!

Jake was confined to his stable, and much to my annoyance, Charlie was shut indoors. Fortunately, the cat flaps had been unlocked, so I could come and go as I pleased. But to keep Charlie out, the bedroom door was shut, which deprived me of prime snoozing space. However, I did, have the satisfaction of knowing that Charlie was trapped. He was much too big for my cat flaps, so had to wait for Tracy to take him for a walk - always on the lead! Charlie had developed a reputation for disobedience!

When the snow cleared, we had a brief Indian Summer, before winter set in with a vengeance towards the end of November. The house became a cold and miserable place, with Jessica and Toby leaving early on weekdays and not returning until late.

Rather than stay inside with Charlie, I roamed the fields and when I felt like a doze, used the tractor seat, which was really quite comfortable.

There was also a place I had discovered in the stable. Jake's enormous body gave off an incredible amount of heat, even if it did pong a bit.

"Hi, Jake." He was looking out through the stable door. His head jerked frantically from left to right. I whispered again. "Hi, Jake. It's me, your favorite cat."

He snorted, backing into the stable, stamping and looking around.

"Up here, Jake." He lifted his head, made that high pitched squealing noise and stood on his hind legs, frantically clawing at the air in an attempt to get at me. But, I was on a ledge above the door, well out of reach. I waited for him to calm down.

" I thought we could be friends."

"I remember what you did to my nose, and I saw what you did to the dog. If you ever get on my back, I'll throw you off and trample on you."

"I'm sure you would," I said evenly. "That's why I have no intention of going there, and I promise you, I only meant to give you a friendly tap on the nose; the claw was a mistake."

He looked up at me with those enormous eyes which held so much love for Jessica but only suspicion for me.

I spoke quickly. "Look, Jake. I know how much you mean to Jessica. She feels the same about me, so it would be good for her if we could get along. I will never scratch you again, that's a promise."

"A promise?"

"Yes, a promise."

What I didn't say was that if I could ever encourage him to eat ragwort - I would. A tabby can't change its stripes!

*****

"Hey! Charlie! What are you doing up here?"

I was having an afternoon nap on the family bed, on a rare day when the bedroom door had been left open, when I heard that big lump of a dog flop down on the bedroom carpet.

He looked up at me. "I was told to stay downstairs?"

Help! He was taking this disobedience business to extremes - and invading my space! I thought quickly.

"Who told you not to come up here?" His eyes went blank.

"Who did you disobey?"

His eyes rolled around. He was thinking. "The mistress - it was the mistress."

"Well," I said, casually moving to the edge of the bed and dropping a paw in front of his face. "From now on the rules are changed, you disobey Toby - but you obey Jessica. Or in doggy language, you disobey your master, but obey your mistress. Understand?" He saw and heard my claws snap out and cowered away.

"Yes - I've got it. I disobey the master, but obey the mistress."

"Sure you've got it Charlie?"

"Yes - I'm sure."

"What are you doing up here then?"

Charlie groaned and hauled himself to his feet. He paused and looked back from the doorway. I could see he was summoning up the courage to ask me a question. Eventually he blurted it out. "Look, I'm not complaining, Lettuce; but why is it always me who has to obey orders?"

"Or disobey," I reminded him before answering his question. "The point is Charlie, and you must never forget this - you are only a dog!

The result of the Baines inquest made the national newspapers and I heard Toby telling Jessica about it, before I received the news from Vince. We were in the kitchen, Jessica sitting at the table having a second cup of coffee, Toby on a bar stool over by the window, reading the newspaper. I was enjoying the warmth of the range cooker, pretending to be asleep. Toby broke the silence.

"Listen to this, Jess. It's a report on the inquest into the Baines drowning." He read from the paper.

"The coroner was minded to record death by misadventure, however a single, deep, unexplained wound on the back of the victim's hand, could have played a part in Mr Baines losing control of the wheelchair and plunging into the fish pond. Had the victim been of slimmer build, even with one leg in plaster, he may have floated clear. As it was, the body was found wedged in the wheelchair, the weight of which, took him down. With no evidence of other human involvement, the coroner recorded an open verdict."

Toby rolled up the newspaper and pointed it at me. "Of course there was no evidence of human involvement, your honor. There is the culprit! That harmless looking tabby is a killer. We have dead bodies strewn outside our back door every morning of the week to prove the point"

Jessica laughed, which was all the encouragement Toby needed. He slid off the bar stool and strode across the kitchen, rolled-up newspaper clutched against one lapel, the thumb of his other hand hooked under the other.

"I put it to you, your honor, that this is all the evidence you need to solve this most heinous of crimes." With a flourish, he unhooked his thumb and extended the back of his hand towards Jessica. "Witness the result of a recent attack from that evil monster. Note the single wound which has yet to heal. I rest my case."

"That's no case!" Jessica playfully pushed his hand away.

"Of course it's a case; look! It's a single wound; and what does it say in the Coroner's Report? He opened the newspaper and read the incriminating sentence. "There was a single, deep, unexplained wound on the back of the victim's hand."

Jessica looked at him suspiciously. "You can't be serious?"

"You bet I'm serious. There have been too many unexplained accidents when that cat has been around."

"Nonsense! Lettuce scratched you because you tried to throw her off the bed. She sank her claws into the back of your hand; hardly life threatening."

"So how do you account for the one deep wound?"

"One of her claws went in deeper than the others. Really, Toby. You must stop this vendetta against Lettuce. What has she done to you?"

"What hasn't she done to me? She's shredded the back of my hands, clawed my arms and my legs, and, bitten my thumb down to the bone.

I opened my eyes and gave a plaintive meow.

"There, you've upset her. Come on, darling, we don't need to listen to this nonsense, let's go and see Jake." She picked me up, and made for the back door, Toby tried to stop us.

"It was only a joke!"

"If it was meant as a joke, we didn't find it funny! Did we darling?"

I said nothing. Toby was getting too close to the truth!

*****

Preparations were being made for Christmas. I had seen it all before, but at Walnut Tree Farm it took on a new dimension. The house was big enough for visitors and judging by the emails flying around, it was going to be a full house over the festive season. Toby put a large Christmas tree in the entrance hall and a smaller one in the lounge. Then he set about putting lights on the trees, which was fair enough, but draping strings of lights on the outside of the house and around the stables, was not to my liking. A bit naff if you ask me.

A stack of presents began to grow under the tree in the lounge. I monitored them on a daily basis, remembering that last year there was one for me, a packet of fancy treats, which were quite disgusting! Toby wanted to watch me open my present, but to maintain my dignity, I walked away. If he thought he could buy my affection with a cheap trinket, he would have to think again!

By Christmas week, the stack of presents had grown to a small mountain. As I idly sorted through them with my computer claw, I counted four for Charlie, but only one for me. I sniffed at it - same as last year - yuk! A large wrapped box caught my attention. It was from Toby to Jessica. I was intrigued, surely not another pet? I sniffed; nothing animal that I could detect; this required further investigation. I pushed my claw under the sealed strip at the back of the wrapping and slowly eased it apart. Intent on completing the task without tearing the wrapping paper, I did not see Toby, peeping through the open door from the kitchen until it was too late. He had seen my computer claw in action and I could tell from the look of triumph on his face, he was sure I had killed Mr Baines!

But it was not that knowledge which signed his death warrant, it was his main Christmas gift for Jessica – TWO KITTENS!

CHAPTER THIRTEEN: THE ULTIMATE BUZZ

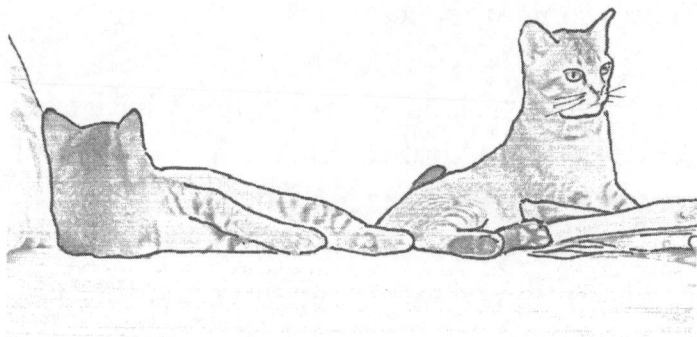

Over Christmas, the kittens, Holly and Mistletoe, were a big hit. What is it with Jessica and names?

Toby tried to implicate me in the death of Mr Baines on several occasions, but visiting relatives and friends laughed it off as a joke. I mounted a charm offensive and visited every lap, apart from Toby's.

Everyone thought I was wonderful, especially towards the kittens, which made Toby's theory ever more risible. But, as I dozed on a chosen lap with a contented look upon my face, I was, as ever, working on Toby's come-uppance.

I had decided against killing Charlie. He was a daft mutt, but couldn't help it, and I had grown to like him, as I had Benton.

Jake, to be honest, was just too big to tackle. Finding enough ragwort to poison him and then put it in a place where he might eat it, was too great a task.

The kittens should be easy meat, but where would the satisfaction be in that?

So I spent my time working hard on that plan for Toby and strangely, two television programs of the many playing in the background throughout the festive season, were to have a profound influence on my plan for his demise.

One was a film about gangsters in a place called New York. They spoke a bit like Vince, and boy, did they have some great ways of killing each other! I sat in a chair, unnoticed as Toby and a friend swapped stories and drank beer. They had seen the film several times before and only paused in their story telling to watch scenes of particular interest. One was so wonderfully horrific, that I decided to use it as a template to warn Toby of my intentions.

"What the ...!"
Toby was about to get into bed and jumped back in horror.

"Look what your darling Lettuce has left under the covers!"

Jessica stirred. I peeped over her recumbent body.

"What's that, darling?"

"Only half a blinking rabbit - that's all."

I wanted to stay to tell him it was not half a rabbit, it was a rabbit's head, but he was furious and showing murderous intent. I scampered down the stairs and as I clattered through the utility room cat flap, decided that if he was too dim to get the message, he deserved the consequences.

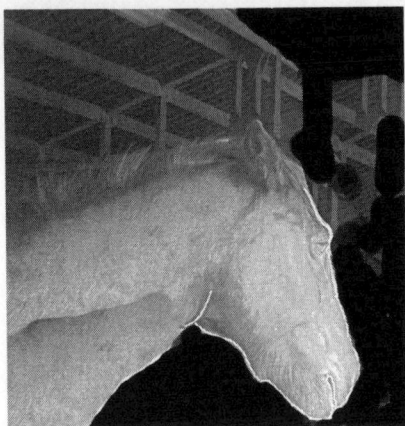

Jake heard me enter the adjoining stable and scrabble along to my ledge.

"What are you up to, Lettuce?"

"I've been kicked out. I'm going to sleep here."

Jake fidgeted nervously. "Look, I'm okay with you being close during the day, part of 'our accord', as you put it, but I do get nervous when you're up there, in the dark, where I can't see you. Anyway, why did they kick you out?"

I told Jake about my warning for Toby, but he to could not understand the significance of a rabbit's head in the bed. When I explained, he kicked off to such an extent that I left the warmth of his stable for the cooler but quieter hay barn and the comforts of the tractor seat.

In the early hours, I heard something moving. I eased myself up in the tractor seat to investigate. It was a rat! It scampered across the hay bales and hesitated before heading across the yard towards the stables: hesitation which proved fatal!

I carried the dead rat to the usual place by the back door and carefully laid it out. I was tempted to take it indoors and drop it accidentally onto the carpet on Toby's side of the bed, but common sense prevailed. My plan for Toby could not be rushed. I had to prepare for his birthday at the end of February.

Hi Little Buddy – Sorry to be the bearer of bad tidings, but our old friend Sandy has bit the dust. Crossed the road once too often and got hit by a car. He was not aurophobic like Snowy. Sandy went direct and quick. Trouble was the car was quicker. Hope all is well with you – Vince.

I was shattered by the news. Sandy was a great one for crossing Bloomfield Road and wandering far and wide. I sent a quick reply.

Hi Vince – Real sorry to hear about Sandy. Must be a great shock to all. Things are not so good here. Toby is a real pain – he bought Jessica two kittens for Christmas and before that brought home a stray dog. This place is getting crowded! Added to that, he suspects my involvement in the drowning of Mr Baines. Saw me using my computer claw over Christmas and wants to prove my guilt. Fortunately everyone here over the holiday thought he was joking and laughed at the idea. But he's determined to take me down, so I've decided it's him or me! Working on a great plan for his demise. Wish me success – Little Buddy.

There was a quick response.

Hi Little Buddy – High time we tried a face to face on Skype. If ya can remember how, switch it on and I'll give ya a call.

I clicked on Skype and waited for his call. Within a minute he was on-screen.

"Hi Vince, great to see you. Can you see me?"

"Sure thing, Little Buddy. Ya look good."

It was the first time we had tried to communicate via Skype. We were perched on chair backs to get on camera. Vince looked genuinely pleased to see me, but came straight to the point.

"I worry about ya, Little Buddy, you're getting paranoid. Toby may suspect ya of having something to do with the Baines death, but believe me, the police will only laugh if he suggests it. You saw that for ya self over Christmas."

His yellow eyes were friendly – concerned, and I felt guilty for not believing. I squirmed uneasily on the narrow top of the chair, not the most comfortable of places.

"Sorry, Vince, but you seem to forget that he's seen my computer claw."

"What he thinks he's seen or not seen, makes no difference. Ya know ya did it. I know ya did it, and Toby thinks he knows ya did it, but if he goes public, he'll become a laughing stock."

"But the claw?"

Vince waved a large dismissive paw.

"Forget it, Little Buddy. As I've said before, human folks don't think we're as clever as dawgs - never have, never will. Use it to your advantage."

I gave him a rueful smile. "Take your point, Vince, but Toby has become a real pain since we moved here. I'm going to have to do something to punish him."

"I'm all for that, Little Buddy, but we'll have to discuss it some other time. The folks are back - keep me posted."

"Cheers, Vince. I'll do that."

The screen went blank, but as I was unlikely to be disturbed, I decided to stay on the computer and do some more research on my idea for Toby's demise. I jumped down from the back of the chair, tapped in BEE KEEPING on the keyboard and hit the search button.

BEE
KEEPING

FOR BEGINNERS

The other TV program Toby showed an interest in over the Christmas holiday, was a documentary about bees and bee keeping. As usual, I was pretending to be asleep at the time, but my ears pricked up when I heard mention that some people can have a life threatening allergic reaction to bee stings.

Subsequent research revealed symptoms of anaphylactic shock: Swelling of the airways - nausea - stomach pain - feeling of doom - unconsciousness - death.

What a way for Toby to go! Just the ticket!

I was tremendously excited until further research revealed that the average person would need to be stung over one thousand times to receive enough bee venom for that to happen. So, that was my challenge. But first I had to work out how Toby would become a bee keeper.

Time and time again, I left the appropriate site page on screen for Jessica, hoping it would promote the idea of a bee keeping kit for Toby's birthday, but she never got the message, Eventually I had to take matters into my own paws.

One day, after placing an order online for a pair of shoes, she left her debit card by the computer. I feigned sleep as she rushed off to ride Jake and as they rode down the lane - I pounced!

The hive and all the bee keeping kit arrived the day after Toby's birthday, which all things considered, was quite good timing. Toby was really pleased, though somewhat baffled when Jessica denied all knowledge of it. She thought Toby had bought it as a present for himself, but liked the idea of a beehive in the orchard, and so it was left at that. I was bitterly disappointed to discover the bees would not be sent until June. I missed that detail in the rush to place the order.

I watched carefully as Toby assembled the hive in the living room and practiced putting frames in and taking them out. He tried on the smock, the round hat with a veil and the long gloves. Jessica found it mildly amusing, but when he wanted to light a fire to test the smoker, she ordered him outside. I sneaked out through the back door to watch and very soon a plan began to hatch.

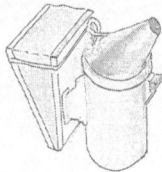

CHAPTER FOURTEEN: IN HASTE

This is the day! Weather hot, Jessica away and Toby unable to resist playing bee keeper.

Everything has come together nicely and I am well hidden in an overhanging branch of an apple tree above the bee hive. On cue, Toby appears wearing his bee keeping smock and round hat with veil. I've sabotaged the veil, and am fairly confident it will split away from the smock, but what I'm really banking on are the holes pierced in the leather bellows of the smoker with my computer claw.

Working the bellows, Toby approaches the hive carefully but fails to notice that there is no smoke coming out of the business end of the smoker.

He wafts it around, lifts the top off the hive, and works the bellows again. Satisfied he stands beneath me, waiting for the smoke to have its calming effect on the bees.

The top of his hat is within range of my computer claw and without hesitation, I strike! In one swift movement the hat is hooked, the veil rips away, and hat and veil are lifted from Toby's head.

Toby panics and drops the smoker into the hive. Bees swarm out and within seconds, Toby's exposed face and neck is smothered in angry bees. Screaming for help, he runs from the orchard towards the stables. Charlie, who is dozing by the tractor, wakes up barking. By this time I am close behind, following Toby into the yard. He makes for Jake's drinking trough and ducks his head and shoulders under water.

Some of the bees cling to his exposed flesh and drown in the process, others re-group in a menacing swarm over the trough. A breakaway squad attack Charlie, who runs off yelping, but the main swarm zoom back to the orchard.

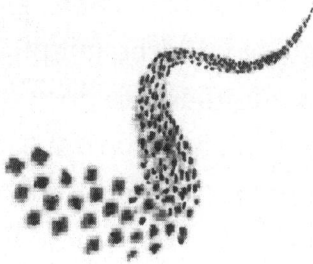

After several seconds, Toby lifts his head, gasps for air, and ducks under again. He repeats the exercise several times, before cautiously looking around. His face is puffed, lips swollen, eyes almost closed. Satisfied the bees have gone, he staggers towards the house. I run the long way round and by the time he drags himself into the kitchen I'm curled up on my favorite chair. He ignores me, as usual, fumbles with the telephone and dials an emergency number. He does it three times before realizing there's no ring tone. He begins to choke and panic, doesn't think to check if the phone is plugged in, which of course it isn't, courtesy of my computer claw!

He's gasping for breath now and searching for his cell phone, but that won't be of any use, not on Walnut Tree Farm. He knows very well that you need to be half a mile up the road to get a signal. He'll never be able to walk 200 yards, let alone half a mile. And Jessica has the car!

I smirk to myself in satisfaction. I've covered every angle.

He drags himself to the door muttering through grotesquely swollen lips. I'm trying to work out what he's mumbling as he stumbles out through the doorway into the garden. Then it clicks, it's - Fergie - Fergie – Fergie. It's the tractor! His only chance and I missed it!

I rush into the library. The computer is on and I hurriedly write this final chapter.

Toby has been trying to start the tractor for some time. It fires and I hear the gears crash as he tries to select reverse to back out of the yard. This is it. This is THE END. It has to be Toby – or Me!

Hi Vince, If you don't hear from me again, the attached document will tell all you need to know.

In haste - Little Buddy.

CATTUS ADDENDUM:

All cats are killers, it's just a matter of degree.
There can be little doubt that little Buddy was
a scheming tabby, but the death of Desmond
Baines was a mistake, even though brilliantly
planned and executed – if you'll excuse the
pun.

The killing of of Toby through
anaphylactic shock was as Machiavellian as
you can get, and it would have been the
perfect crime, except for one thing – a dog!
Little Buddy underestimated Charlie! When
she went out into the yard after sending the
email, she found Toby slumped over the
tractor steering wheel. The engine was
running, but Toby was going nowhere. She
could see he would never make it up the road
to get a signal for his cell phone. All she had to
do was wait for him to breathe his last.

Then she heard barking and a screech of
brakes. She ran to the farm entrance and saw
Charlie, standing in front of a car about 100
yards up the lane.

The driver hooted on the car horn. Charlie retreated down the lane, but as the car got going, he turned and barking like mad, blocked its path again, The car came to a jolting halt, the driver hooted and Charlie repeated the process, much to the annoyance of the driver, until the car was abreast the entrance to Walnut Tree Farm. At that point Charlie would not budge. No matter how much the driver hooted, he just kept on barking. Eventually the driver got the message, followed Charlie up the drive and found Toby slumped over the steering wheel on the tractor.

Toby survived. Charlie was a hero and evidence of bee stings on his ears and nose made him more so. Little Buddy disappeared and Jessica was upset by the thought that her darling Lettuce had been attacked by bees, ran off to get away from them and died a horrible lonely death in a ditch. She spent weeks, scouring the country side on Jake.

At the onset of winter, there was word in our neighborhood that a stray cat had turned up at Sandy's old house and ingratiated itself with his folks. I went along with Ting Ling to investigate and was mighty pleased I did. The stray was a tabby, a tabby which was immediately accepted by all cats on the Bloomfield Estate as having - REPUTATION!

As Ting Ling put it. "All tabby cat look same - and yet - not same."

Welcome home, Little Buddy.

Vince